Lucy N. A Kelsey

The September Holocaust

a record of the great forest fire of 1894

Lucy N. A Kelsey

The September Holocaust
a record of the great forest fire of 1894

ISBN/EAN: 9783337255275

Printed in Europe, USA, Canada, Australia, Japan

Cover: Foto ©Andreas Hilbeck / pixelio.de

More available books at **www.hansebooks.com**

The
September Holocaust

A RECORD OF
THE GREAT FOREST FIRE
OF 1894

BY
ONE OF THE SURVIVORS

Light is our sorrow for it ends to-morrow,
  Light is our death that cannot hold us fast;
So brief a sorrow can be scarce a sorrow,
  Or death be death so quickly past.
                              —*Christina Rossetti.*

MINNEAPOLIS:
ALFRED ROPER PRINTING CO., PRINTERS,
1894.

To the Brother,

MORE THAN KIND,

WHOSE ENCOURAGEMENT HAS GIVEN

INSPIRATION

TO THIS LITTLE VOLUME,

IT IS INSCRIBED

BY

The Author.

CONTENTS.

PREFACE.

The events recorded in this little book have the merit of painstaking exactness, and confirm the old adage that "truth is stranger than fiction."

Without attempt at artistic embellishment, the writer has displayed a rare genius in pleasantly picturing the peacefulness of the settlement in the forest, the wild, rugged beauty of this new country, the hardships of the pioneer, and the contentment of those who for a time, must brave all, in order to make themselves new homes.

Who can measure the hope that lightens labor, that fills the soul with expectant blessings?

Then the recital of that awful catastrophe—so vivid, so graphic. Such a portrayal could only be written by one who had passed through the fiery furnace of flame.

In a world scarred by graves, and hallowed by sacred memories, is it any wonder that we pause, amid the rush and whirl of business, to listen to the tread of hurrying feet, and read, in faces upturned, life's lesson spelled out for good or ill?

Is it any wonder that we pause when disaster, awful and

appalling, visits us, to find instinctively, that humanity is bound together in bonds of unselfish helpfulness?

So in these pages, grateful acknowledgement is made by one who speaks for all.

When in the coming years, this burnt wilderness shall have been changed into beautiful farms and made to "blossom as the rose," and you, dear reader, shall pass en-route between the Twin Cities and Duluth, think of that day when the "heavens were rolled together as a scroll, and the elements melted with fervent heat."

C. W. H.

The September Holocaust.

CHAPTER I.

INCIDENTS BY THE WAY.

Our train left the Union Depot at 1:30 p. m., one day in the latter part of July.

It was one of the extreme days for which the hot, dry summer of 1894 will be long remembered.

I had with me only the two youngest boys, as my husband and oldest boy had preceded me to our new location.

My fourteen-year-old daughter had been left for a few weeks at her old home, and her little sister in the city.

We were traveling on the Eastern Minnesota division of the Great Northern, and after passing Elk River the indications were that showers had been much more frequent than in the vicinity of the Twin Cities.

On we sped, through a fertile country that was losing familiar characteristics, and soon we found ourselves on the border of the pine district.

After leaving Princeton we rode into smoky atmosphere caused by smoldering forest fires.

Nowhere at that time did we see flames, but at intervals it was evident that the woods were burning slowly.

Once our train came to a sudden halt between stations. "What is the trouble?" was the inquiry. "A tree has fallen across the track."

Putting my head out of the window I saw a relay of men lifting the tree, and as it was not very large they were able in a few moments to swing it one side and the train moved on.

We were on the Limited. At the ticket office on Nicollet avenue I had been informed that I could go up to Hinckley and ride back eight miles, or stop over night at Milaca and go on to Brook Park, my destination, the next day.

As neither prospect seemed alluring I resolved to trust to the good nature of the conductor, and rested quietly in the conviction that I should not go on to Hinckley that day.

After passing Mora I was ready to gather up my belongings at a moment's notice.

The twelve miles remaining were quickly passed over, and in less time than it takes to tell it I was standing with the little ones by the side of the track and our train had disappeared.

At Hinckley, the next station of importance, the Great Northern forms a junction with the St. Paul & Duluth road.

Hinckley was a town of about 1,200 inhabitants,

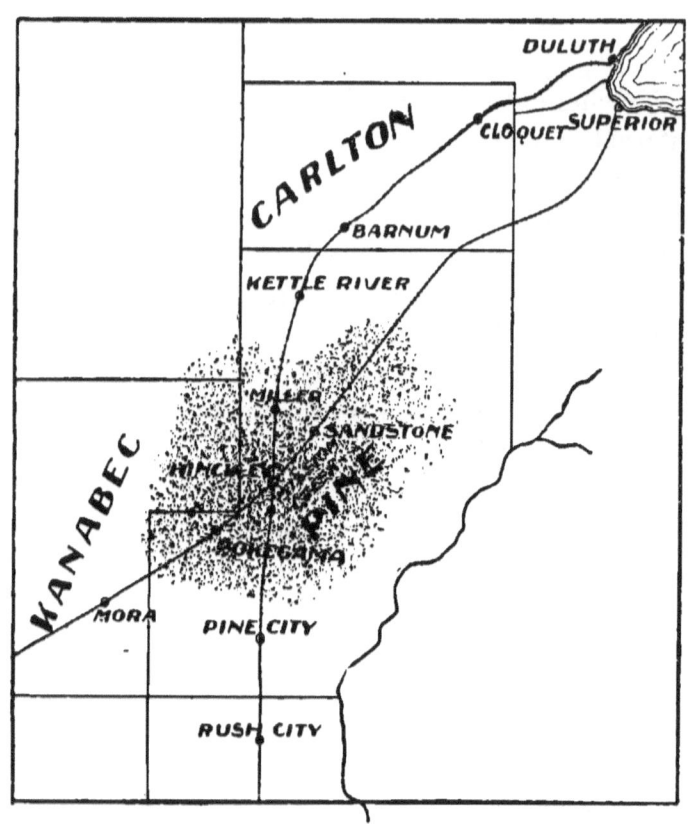

THE BURNED DISTRICT OR MAP OF PINE COUNTY.

of which the principal industry was the Brennan
Lumber Co.'s saw and planing mills.

The Eastern Minnesota from that point runs in a
northeasterly direction, through Sandstone, crossing
Kettle River, and continues its course to Superior,
thence to Duluth.

The St. Paul & Duluth line, which is more direct,
after passing the little town called Mission Creek,
runs into Hinckley, thence north through Miller,
then Kettle River and northeast to Duluth. Sandstone was a town of four or five hundred people,
while Mission Creek was a small settlement, consist-
ing of the inevitable saw mill, common to all these
towns in Pine county, and beside railway buildings, only a few dwellings. Brook Park was at that
time, a promising little settlement southwest of the
prosperous town of Hinckley, having been settled
mainly within a year's time.

To my surprise, I seemed to have been left to
one side of the main settlement, how far, I knew
not. Before me stretched the interminable track.

Across a side track was a pair of closed bars, and
within, a wagon road wound away among the trees.
Near by was a small building about six feet square.

"I thought we were coming up north," complained little Earl.

"We are up north surely, and perhaps we will
find some one, if we keep up courage."

I was in doubt whether to go through the bars

on an uncertainty, or walk up the railroad track towards a house that seemed nearly a mile away.

Deciding finally on the latter course, I gathered up my burdens and we started on. As we proceeded, I found that we were nearer the main settlement than I at first supposed.

Before me stretched a high trestle bridge, and just beyond, the house first described, which I afterward found was occupied by Mr. Nelson and family.

As we neared the trestle, at our left and approached by passing over a log dam, was a steam saw mill.

At our right, not far away, was a large new frame building, the boarding house.

In reaching this we passed close by some low log huts in which three or four families were dwelling temporarily, while deciding on permanent location.

Beyond, among the trees was "the store" and "post office" kept by Mr. Berg, whose family occupied rooms adjoining.

The kindly hostess at the boarding house met me at the door.

"Will you take in some wayfarers?" said I, giving her my name.

"Oh, yes," she said, cordially. "Your husband will soon be here."

This gentleman soon appeared, and at the supper table I met three single men, who were known familiarly as John, Frank and Charlie. The table was well supplied with proofs of Mrs. Carver's good cooking, and all did justice to her skill.

After a good night's rest, we were ready to explore the settlement.

Our first trip was through the woods to the Doctor's.

A single path had been cut through the trees, a path which wound in zig-gag fashion over and around obstructions, in the way of stumps and large logs, which we mounted or went around.

We came in a few moments to a clearing. At the right, and near by, was the foundation for a substantial school house.

"There is Mr. Ward, at work," said Meb, the Doctor's elder daughter, who was showing us the way, "and here is our garden. Does it not look fine?"

Across the creek, to our left, it lay, in flourishing condition; corn, cabbages, beets, and potatoes, contrasting favorably with one I had left fast drying up at my home near the city.

Here we caught another glimpse of Mr. Nelson's house close to the railroad.

"What beautiful evergreens!" I exclaimed, as we again entered the woods.

"Yes, there are many about our home, and over the creek to the northwest, is our village park."

"There seems to be an endless variety of trees here," said I, as we went onward.

"Papa has found sixteen different varieties just about our home." Most conspicuous among these were the graceful fir balsam, towering pine, and sturdy elm.

"Now you have the first glimpse of the house," said Meb, and among the slender poplars, maples and evergreens it appeared, still unfinished, but looking homelike, with a hammock swung before the door, and screens at doors and windows.

"Mother, here is auntie and the little boys," announced Meb, and my sister and the "princess" gave us affectionate greeting.

"You did not bring Maidie with you I see, auntie," said "the princess," who came in Maytime, and was now fifteen.

"No, she remained behind to pack houshold goods and see that they are sent when we are ready for them. Meantime I will remain at the boarding house and superintend building matters."

The Doctor's people were only camping down for the summer, having left most of their furniture at their old home.

Books, newspapers, easy chairs, and a few rugs and fans, helped all to pass the time comfortably and sociably.

"Who will show you the way to your new home?" asked my sister, as after a pleasant visit we bade

them "Good bye," and started back to the boarding house. "I think I shall call on Allen for that
service, as his father will probably be too busy," I
replied.

On our return I met "Jakey," a young Jew.   I
saw him often afterward and found him to be an in-
telligent and industrious young man.

At ten o'clock the next morning, Allen appeared
and we walked down a wagon road, which led east
from the boarding house, passed the school house
site, and turned into a path cleared through the
brush, bordered at first by young maples, raspberry
bushes and various kinds of undergrowth.

Following this, occasionally stepping over fallen
logs, we found the woods growing thicker, our path
more narrow, the ground spongy, and balsam and
pine trees growing denser, forming interlacing arch-
es over our heads.   In some places the trees were
so near together it was like twilight, although the sun
was shining brightly.   Here it was delightfully cool,
while ferns, brakes, mosses and other growth pecu-
liar to marshy places sprung up about us.

Further on were open spaces bordered by beautiful and symmetrical evergreens at different stages
of growth; then we reached a bed of low brakes,
extending under the trees as far as we could see,
the delicate sprays so frail and lovely that even little
Lyle noticed them and said, "How pretty, mamma!"
This we named "the evergreen path."

We soon reached a road running at right angles to the path. "Out of the byway into the highway." Turning eastward and stubbing along over roots and grubs for quite a distance, at last Earl, who was a little ahead, where the road made an abrupt turn, shouted, "Mamma, mamma, I see the house."

In a moment more we emerged from the woods and found ourselves standing in a clearing in about the middle of which stood our future home.

The house, which was constructed of solid blocks hewed from logs of pine, ash, tamarack and basswood, faced the south, and in the east end was a door, over which in the gable above was a double window. There was a door in the south side as well, and large windows in the west and in the north and south sides.

The trees had all been cut down south of the house to a distance of several rods. To the east the trees were blackened and many of them dead. A brush fire had got beyond control a few weeks before and had burned many of them.

To the north and west, the trees were only a few steps from the house.

Though at first glance it seemed as if we were surrounded on all sides by an impenetrable forest, I soon found a romantic logging road, winding through balsams, pines and tamaracks as well as other native trees. The trees arched here so prettily that we called it the "arched road." This road opened

out into a beautiful meadow, through which flowed
a creek, now nearly dry in places. There was a
shorter road to the meadow through the blackened°
trees east, but this became the favorite path.

My husband called it a fifteen-minute walk to the
post office from our place, but with the little ones
to help over rough places I think it usually took me
twenty-five minutes. From time to time I met the
settlers on my walks to and fro, or had better op-
portunities for making their acquaintance when
they dropped into the boarding house.

Mrs. Baty came in about four o'clock one afternoon to spend an hour with Mrs. Carver. She was
the wife of one of the proprietors of the mill, keeping house for the summer in a little frame building
near Mr. Nelson's. She was expecting to return
to her pleasant home in Wisconsin in a few weeks,
so did not greatly enjoy her unsettled sojourn in
this place. I had already met Mr. Baty, who as
well as his partner, Mr. Seymour, were very social
and friendly.

Mr. Baty was an old woodsman, ready for a hunt
at any time, and always willing to answer my numer-
ous questions in regard to matters in which I had
become interested since coming into the woods.

A good share of the milk for the settlement was
brought by Nora, a sister of Mrs. Anderson. She
was a bright little girl, modest and faithful, and her
pleasant ways quite won our hearts.

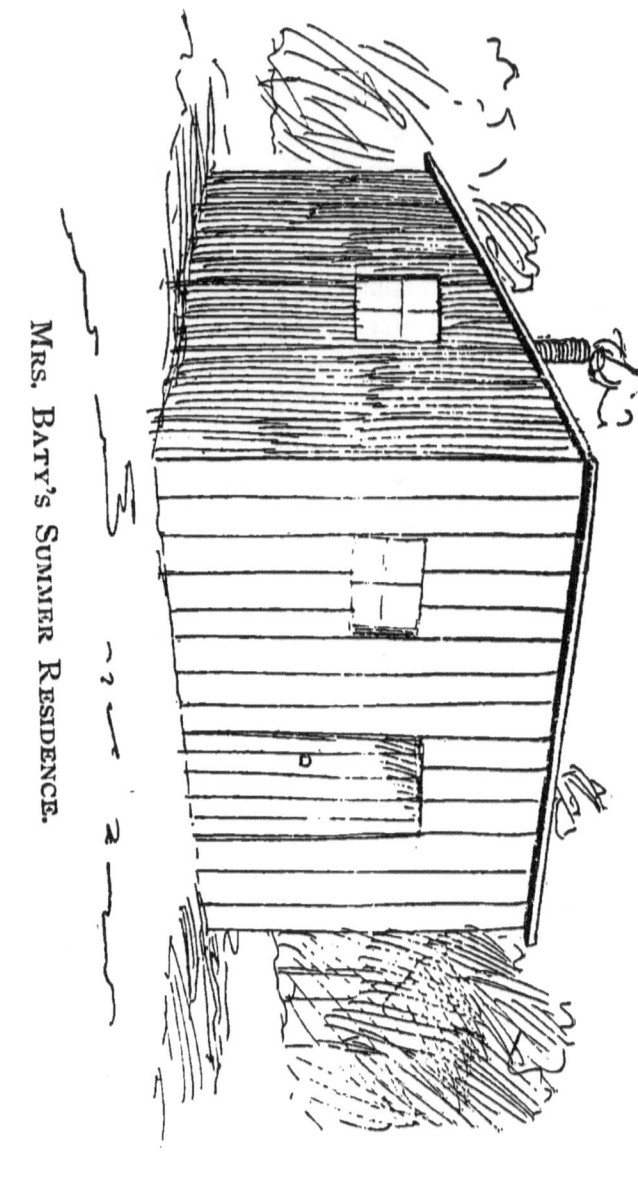

MRS. BATY'S SUMMER RESIDENCE.

The nearest of the low log houses was occupied by Mr. France and family. The father and son Dave, who was the oldest of six boys, were musicians, and as dusk came on we were usually entertained by a duet on violin and dulcimer.

Mr. and Mrs. Braman and their son Jay occupied the adjoining house, while the remainder were occupied by Jewish families.

During the first week of my stay, Mr. Carver brought in a large pail nearly full of raspberries. Wishing to put up some of the fruit, I started one morning with the little boys, on my quest.

Nora was just returning from her rounds with the milk, so we walked on together. Crossing the track near the trestle bridge, we opened bars, went over the log dam, past the mill and stables and turned into a fairly well traveled wagon road.

After some time we passed Mr. Thompson's house. "I should think Mr. Thompson would get lonely 'baching it' here," I remarked.

"He is not alone," said Nora, "for Mr. Gonyea stays with him. Mr. Gonyea's family are still at their home in Kettle River." "There are some raspberries over there" she continued, indicating a place a short distance from us. "I must go on."

"How far away does your sister live?"

"Not very far from here."

"Have you any near neighbors?"

"Mrs. Molander and Mrs. Raymond are quite near us."

Saying "good bye," she soon disappeared among the trees. After a rather unsuccessful search, I returned, as the children were tired and it was growing very warm.

A week after my arrival, there was a fire west of us, three miles away, and Mr. Collier's house was in danger.

"Nearly every man in town is down fighting fire," said Mr. Carver. "They are going to bring Mrs. Collier, her mother and the little ones here for fear they will be suffocated by the smoke. Mrs. Collier is sick, and they will have to bring her on a bed."

In a short time they arrived, and we found them a pleasant addition to our family.

Little two-year-old Vernon was a great favorite with all. He talked very little and his call for water "all yi," seemed very odd.

At that time the smoke was often so thick as to show plainly in our rooms at night. In time, however, the threatened danger was averted, and in about a week, Mr. Collier's family returned to their home.

"I do not think we need to be greatly alarmed about fires," said Doctor one day. "They burn very slowly and we can, with care, control them."

The work of clearing brush and stumps and fallen trees was vigorously pushed by those who were not busy haying.

CHAPTER II.

CHARACTERISTICS OF SETTLERS.

"We have been here just two weeks to-day," I said to Mrs. Carver, as I stood by the window and watched the train switch back and forth. "I would not be surprised if our household goods had come."

An hour or two later my boy brought word that our furniture was on the side track in a box car. "Run down and tell your father; I think he would like to know at once." In a short time Allen came back out of breath, saying, "I am to hunt up Charlie Olson, ask him to hitch up, and bring a load at once. I think he is down among the tamaracks."

"Where are they?"

"Back of Mr. Berg's place.

"I will go with you and help find him."

South of the boarding house, a half a mile or so, we found Charlie, and he put up his scythe at once, and started to the stables.

The little boys and I hurried to the house to be ready for the first load.

Our goods were soon brought, and after two days' time we began to feel a little settled. By Sunday we could rest in a comparatively orderly home.

Monday morning my husband announced, "I must

leave the work here now, and help on the school house. I have put them off too long already. We must get our building in shape for school by the middle of September at latest."

For the next three weeks, he, with Mr. Seymour, Mr. Baty and his son Frank, Mr. Gonyea and occasionally others, worked steadily on the school house.

By the first of September the work was nearly completed, and it was expected that school would soon be in session.

Mr. Seymour, of the mill, superintended the work, and on my walks to and fro I often dropped in to see how the work progressed.

The building was two stories in height, the lower floor divided into schoolroom, hall and cloakroom, which when completed made a very pleasant and commodious addition to our little settlement.

Meantime our own home, though not completed, was very comfortable for warm weather. Stairway and other conveniences must wait.

Our well had been dug by Jakey sometime before we moved in. He had made it "good and large," and the red clay formed a fine solid curbing. The water came in at eight feet. He went down about twelve feet, and we were supplied with clear, pleasant-tasting water, easily drawn by means of a pail to which a rope was attached. This well was southeast of the house, and a little beyond stood "our pine," about one hundred feet high, towering above the surrounding trees.

My husband had covered the well with a platform of pine, with closely fitting cover.

Our potato field was in the southeast corner of the farm and it was a long walk from the house. As I did not like to have Allen go so far away from home alone, I usually went with him, till his sister came. The trip took full two hours, most of the way through the meadow. The haying was over and there were many stacks to be passed on the way.

A great many were busy at that time burning about their stacks, as the hay represented a great deal of work and was very valuable to our settlers.

We were becoming interested in our neighbors and in noting the different ways they had of interesting and occupying themselves in this new and rather wild country.

Mr. Ward was outspoken, yet kind hearted and helpful in any emergency. He and his wife and boy had made great progress in clearing about their home.

We found Mr. Berg very kind and accommodating, just now very busy in plastering and repairing his house and store, that he might be in good shape for cold weather. His wife was a true helpmeet, though frank in her objections to the hardships and inconveniences incident to the life of a pioneer. Those who sit in comfortable homes, surrounded by all the amenities that modern civilization can produce, can have no adequate conception of what it means to be deprived of these comforts. To one reared in cities or large towns, the hardships of necessity seem greater when contrasted with the conveniences enjoyed in past years.

Among the number of those to whom these privations seemed of less weight than to some others, Mrs. Frame may be included. Acknowledging herself to be unusually healthy and hardy, she proved this, by the way she endured life for the present in one room, as rough inside as out. Her ready cheerfulness made light of all inconveniences, and the days found her busily washing, mending and cooking for her family of six sturdy boys.

Mr. Thompson accepted all privations cheerfully, working with a will to build for himself a home. John, Frank and Charlie were of the same material, gifted with genuine grit, undaunted by obstacles, and undismayed by privations.

Mr. Collier found in his wife a good pioneer and one who would bear a willing hand in the struggle to win home and its dear delights from the wilderness about them.

Mrs. Raymond, true to her social nature, made her home attractive to all its inmates and to those who were only guests. The Doctor's large, genial nature won him friends among all classes, while his family formed a pleasant, hospitable center.

Mrs. Nelson's motherly nature was evident in her own home, and the girls, though kept very busy, found time to add their part to the social life that was gradually developing, though at times under unfavorable circumstances.

There was yet no suitable or convenient place for gatherings. No Sunday service, not even Sunday school was held; but many looked forward to the completion of the school house as a fortunate day for this young settlement. There were many no doubt who only felt themselves transient dwellers among us until the time when they could welcome their families and feel that home was here.

One day, I with the little boys explored the meadow in the opposite direction from that we took in going to our potato field. I was delighted with the grand and beautiful scenery in that direction. Afterward when describing my walk to the family, my husband remarked, "You would have reached the doctor's potato field if you had kept on a little farther." Thinking it would be much more interesting to find another way of reaching the doctor's, I with the children, set out one day, having this as a definite purpose.

Striking into our highway west of the house, we went on past the entrance to "the evergreen path," and a few minutes' farther walk brought us to the meadow. Crossing the creek, we walked up the meadow for a time through the closely cropped grass. Our path finally led into the woods near an Indian trail that later I was told was the road that led to Pine City.

We soon emerged from the woods again, finding ourselves on the borders of the potato field where Carlton and Willie were busy at work. "This is a new way for us, boys," I said. "What is our best path to the house?" "Keep on between the rows and cross the creek on a board you will see over that way," indicating the direction. The creek was deeper here than at any other place we had seen, but we crossed safely and soon found ourselves under the trees. My sister was reclining in the hammock, and bidding her keep her comfortable position, I sat on the doorstep as we chatted.

"I expect Maidie on the 4:20 train to-morrow afternoon," I said to "the princess," who joined us. "Shall we go together and meet her?" "I shall be glad to," said "the princess." "We will meet at Mrs. Carver's then at a little after four." At the appointed time we met and as the train came in were rewarded by seeing our expected passenger. After a short call at the Doctor's we escorted the little maid to her new home, where she soon found a great deal to interest her and occupy her time.

Some weeks later, my sister sent over word one

day that her young people were going out for cranberries and would like to have Allen and Maidie join them.

"How far will you have to go before you reach the marsh?" we asked Carlton, who brought the message.

"Not much more than a mile, I believe," said he.

"Is it not early in the season to pick them?"

"They will not be very ripe, but the Indians have been in the habit of coming in the fall and taking them, so papa thinks we had better go early."

"I suppose they ripen after being picked?"

"Yes."

"When are you going?"

"Just after dinner."

"Well, I will let the children join you."

They went that day and the next, getting about eighteen quarts of the fruit, which we spread in the sun to ripen. After that we heard of different parties going out for cranberries, and concluded the Indians would be disappointed when they came later.

I suggested to Meb one day that I might join them the next time they went out. "I think you had better leave it all to us young folks," said she. "They grow so low that it is very tiresome to pick them."

Cranberry sauce, pie and jelly were added to our table fare at this time. We were fortunate in getting a fine quality of flour, and in fact had no reason to complain of the supplies our friend Mr. Berg brought in for us.

CHAPTER III.

ENTERPRISE AND PUSH.

The amount of work done in the past six months
in this new settlement had been great indeed,
though as the farms were so shut off from each
other by the dense forest growth, it was impossible
to see what had been accomplished as in places
more compactly built. Messrs. Seymour and Baty
had brought in machinery and put up their mill early
in the spring. The mill was idle just now, as all
the men were busy haying or protecting their hay,
or putting up shelter for themselves and families.
Occasionally those who were sportsmen found opportunity for a few hours' hunt. All were too busy
to haul logs. More teams were expected later, and
cows, of which there was at present a great scarcity, were to be brought in also. The ground until
late in the spring had been soaked with water, and
the flats near the creek at that time were over-
flowed.

A more cheerful band of pioneers, however, could
not be found. All were enterprising and industrious, yet their discomforts and hardships were very
serious at times.

The blue joint grass was very fine, standing when
it attained its growth, forty to fifty inches high. A

large amount of hay had been cut and stacked. As all were unwilling to face the prospect of their hard labor going up in flames, strenuous and constant efforts were made to protect the stacks from fire.

Many who had families were now busy in preparing to make their houses comfortable for the winter.

My husband had put in a large field of potatoes, expecting to harvest nearly two hundred bushels. The dry weather more or less affected the crop, and he finally dropped his expectations to half that number. The potatoes were large and of fine flavor, keeping us supplied with as good an article in that line as we could wish.

The boarding house was bright and spotlessly kept, and seemed a haven to the weary plodders who sometimes returned only once a week to its hospitable fare, many of the single men keeping house in the comfortless fashion, which was their only choice, between times. Good Mrs. Carver made each one feel that he was the special object of her interest and care. Though she complained of a scarcity of material, her table was always loaded with wholesome food, deliciously cooked and presented in an appetizing manner. Mr. Carver was her right hand man and had a pleasant word for every one. They were both happy to have little children about them and dispensed kind words and favors to them without stint. Their own little grandsons were very dear to both, and they were looking forward with great pleasure to a visit from them a little later.

Mr. Nelson's people were so near that in the first weeks of my stay I often saw merry little Minnie and her brother Elmer, who was younger. One evening just after supper two children appeared at the door. We looked at them with a puzzled air. "Who are they?" The mystery was soon solved and we all had a hearty laugh. Minnie and Elmer had exchanged clothes, hence the strangeness. Elmer made a rather bashful little girl, but Minnie seemed as much at home in her cap, with hair tucked under it, jacket and knee pants as if she were used to such a dress.

Mr. Berg's people had come in January and having endured many hardships before the warm weather came on, were happy in the prospect of a clean, comfortable as well as warm house. Their repairs had occupied nearly the whole of August and were about completed.

One day on my way home with the mail I stopped at Mrs. Carver's door a few moments. She was looking tired. "You work too hard I'm afraid," I said, thinking the beautifully white floors pleasant to see, but not the weary look in her face. "Have you a large family at present?"

"Not very large now," she replied; "but we received word to-day that a party from Rush City would be here to-morrow. I shall try and find place for them all."

"How many are coming?"

"About three or four couples, I think."

Later, I heard that they remained over one night, returning in the afternoon of the next day.

The outlook for the company, the mill and other interests was at that time very good. The school house would soon be finished, the school in operation, and a new store was being talked of by parties who thought of purchasing the boarding house and finishing it. Logs were to be furnished for the mill and a new impetus was expected, as settlers would no doubt be coming in in the fall.

Calling in to see my sister one day she said, "Doctor is getting ready a collection for the State Fair."

. "I have heard so," I said. "I suppose he will soon make arrangements to go to St. Paul."

"Yes, and I am thinking of going with him, while our house is being plastered and finished. I have a plan I wish to submit to you. I have been thinking of asking you to keep the boys and their sister while we are away."

"I will be glad to have them come."

"We will consider it settled then, shall we?"

"Yes; how soon will you go?"

"Within two weeks."

Maidie clapped her hands when she heard this,

saying, "Now I will have 'the princess' for a whole week and perhaps more."

"You will be coming back about the time I expect little Flo," I said to my sister. "Will you look after her?"

"Yes, willingly," was her reply; so I was well pleased and greatly relieved.

We were enjoying a quiet Sunday afternoon, when Doctor came in and joined us. Suddenly John appeared at the door with the news that there was a fire down by "Big Joe's." "Would the doctor come and help?" "Big Joe," as he was called to distinguish him from "Little Joe," had been hard at work on his place and now the fire threatened to come in and wipe out everything. I had been urging the doctor to stay and take tea with us, but now he must hurry home, don his working suit and go to "Big Joe's" relief. John waited till he returned and they hurried away through the woods toward the southeast. By night the fire was subdued and all was safe.

I found doctor one day busily at work, with a bottle of shellac in one hand and a small brush in the other.

"That chair is quite pretty as well as solid," said I, pausing to watch his motions.

"I think so; see the grain in this," displaying a section of a large log he had just put some finishing touches to. "This is the top of my center table."

"How many pieces will you have in your parlor set?"

"Five or six."

"It will be quite unique, but it must be a great deal of work."

"Yes, this is very solid wood to work in."

"What else will you display at the fair?"

"Specimens of our large vegetables and native woods."

"You should try and have a collection of leaves."

"They would look very pretty, that's a fact, and give a good idea of the many varieties of native trees here."

"I will try and mount some for you, giving the botanical as well as common name."

"Good, I shall like that. You must get the boys to help you."

"I shall need help. Some of the leaves are far beyond my reach. My boy is a great climber."

"Yes, Allen is quite an athlete for a young boy."

"He already has a trapeze under the trees near the house. Have you had to fight fires lately?" I inquired.

"No; I have had a good chance to rest."

"You do not think the mill is in any danger from the south, do you? It seems well cleaned out a long distance beyond."

"Yes, I think it is pretty safe."

"There is a good deal that is combustible about

there. I believe it would be a good plan to burn up everything that cannot be utilized, after our showers."

"That will lessen the danger, surely, in case of a high wind."

"Allen and his father had two great brush fires the other night after the rain. They looked grand, but I hated to think that they were burning after we retired. In the morning they were all out, though I expected to find a fire still."

"We must watch such fires very carefully. Have you seen our stump puller at work?"

"Yes; I was very much interested. There has been one at work down our way and it pulls up trees, roots and all."

"It is a curious sight to see those immense roots sticking straight up in the air."

"It must have been a very heavy wind that would cause such an upheaval."

"Yes, indeed."

"Do you account for it in any other way?"

"Hardly; I suppose hurricanes pass through the woods occasionally and uproot some of those tall trees, strongly rooted as they seem."

"Do you think it is a good plan, Doctor, for our boys to run over that trestle?"

"No, two of them have fallen through. They had better keep away."

"I saw a boy fishing in the pond near the bridge one day. I suppose there are not many fish there."

"No; they don't amount to much. There is a hole there eighteen to twenty feet deep."

"That's a bad place for a boy to wade in, I should think."

"Yes, I have cautioned the boys about it."

"Strange there should be such a hole, and just across from Mr. Nelson's I crossed over the creek on sand and stones and hardly wet my shoes. What do they dump all that refuse from the mill down there for? Such a pile of chips and boards would burn a long time if fire got in there."

"But we do not mean to let it get in. We can run no risks so near our settlement."

CHAPTER IV.

OUR NEIGHBORS.

"We never see the sun rise here," said Allen one morning. "When we were on the prairie in Dakota we never missed it."

"There could not be a greater contrast than these woods are to the open prairie," I remarked.

It was more foggy than usual that morning, or fog and smoke blended to an unusual degree, for we could hardly see dim outlines of the trees nearest the house. Baby Lyle came to me saying, "Isn't God good, mamma? He has cut down all the trees in the night. Now we can see the trains."

"Oh, Lyle," said his sister, "the trees are all there and when the sun shines we will see them again." There was a disappointed look on the little face as he ran off to play, for seeing the trains was a great pleasure to him.

As the days went by a blue haze was always to be seen in the south and east, and occasionally in the north, yet the smouldering fires seemed so far away that we felt no uneasiness. One evening during the second week of my stay the men were talking about a fire they said was about a mile away. I could get little idea of distances, for what others spoke of as a mile seemed to me two or more. I was talking with Aunty Braman at the time and said to her, "Let us walk down that way and see if we can see flames."

"I am willing," she replied; so we walked slowly down the road past Mr. Berg's, the road I had first discovered behind the bars the day of my arrival. We walked half a mile or more without seeming to be any nearer the fire or more affected by the smoke, and met doctor and several others returning with brooms and sacks. "We were going down to see the fire," we said.

"You cannot get very near on this side on account of the dense smoke. We have left it safe for the night." So we turned about and returned with them.

The doctor and his helpers were hard at work for days, clearing out brush and making fire breaks south and west of the boarding house and other buildings on the edge of the settlement. The boys too were faithful workers, earning by hours of work, an occasional afternoon off, when they, with Allen, enjoyed as boys do, freedom to roam about at their own will. There was a great deal to interest them in the woods, and they were learning unconsciously from Nature's great open book.

"Maidie" and "the princess" found opportunity to see each other every day, and Mabel Nelson was often with them. The girls preferred the meadow to "the evergreen path" usually, but about this time

Doctor and his boys made a short cut from their house to the path and this came to be the favored walk to and fro. The only serious impediment was a great log which had to be climbed over near the house. A helping hand here was greatly appreciated.

About ten o'clock one morning Allen came in with a package in his hand. "Mamma," said he, "just guess what I have here."

"A rabbit," said I at a venture.

"No, it is some bear meat. Mr. Seymour shot a bear yesterday about five miles away. He told papa to send round to Mr. Nelson's and get a piece of it. So I went and here it is."

"We must have some for dinner," said his sister.

"I think there will be time to cook it if it is young and tender." So we put our portion of Mr. Bear over to stew and by noon it was nicely cooked.

> "Mr. Finney and his wife,
> They both sat down to sup,
> And they ate, and they ate
> Till they ate the bear meat up,

sang my little cook as we gathered around the table. Our dinner talk that day as well as our dinner savored of bear.

"If you were going through a dark wood and should see a lion on one side and a bear on the other which would you rather, the *lion* would eat you, or the *bear?*"

The question was put to Allen, but his sister interposed with, "which would you rather, the lion would eat *you* or the *bear?*"

"The bear, of course," said Allen, seeing the point quickly.

"They say that the bear has a foot extremely like a man's hand," said their father.

"There is a point for the evolutionists," I remarked. "Perhaps it is 'the missing link.'"

"Our teacher last year thinks that evolution will soon be taught in the schools," said Maidie. "He says that we all descended from savages, and possibly from apes and monkeys."

"I should call that *descent*, and yet Drummond writes of the *ascent* of man."

"There seems to be a number of theories on that subject," I continued. "Drummond thinks that evolution is God's plan of creation, while many of the evolutionists are materialists. Others think that there is nothing in it at all, that God created man in his own image at once, and there were no intermediate steps."

"It is a puzzling question and about as obscure as Emerson."

"But Emerson is not always obscure. I found something of his the other day that even Allen could understand."

"What was it, mamma?"

"When duty whispers low 'thou must,' the youth replies, 'I will.' "

"I think I do understand it," said the boy.

From this we returned to the subject from which we had strayed so far, and meanwhile piled up long slender bones on our plates.

"What fun it must be to hunt," said Allen. "I wish I could have a gun."

"You are too young, my boy. Mrs. Carver could tell you a sad story of her boy, who by means of a gun lost his life. He was older than you, I think."

"Frank Baty shot four times at a deer the other day."

"Where was he?"

"Up in a tree."

"Then he missed the deer after all, did he?"

"Yes."

"How disappointed he must have been!"

"John Powers saw a deer and fawn just south of our house near the edge of the clearing," said his papa. "It was while we were working on the house, before I came one morning."

"Oh, I wish I could see one now," said Allen, looking through the window toward the place indicated.

"I saw some deer tracks in the sand of the creek yesterday."

"Perhaps they come there to get water."

"They don't get much there now. It has nearly all dried up."

"I heard a pack of coyotes yelping as they ran down the valley a night or two ago," said my husband.

"What time of night?" I asked.

"About four o'clock. Mrs. Baty heard them too."

"I am very glad I did not hear them. I don't think it would be a pleasant sound to hear in the night."

"I suppose you went off to sleep again, papa? I don't believe I would have slept a wink the rest of the night," said "Maid Marian."

"I heard Mr. Baty say there was a kind of wild cat that prowled about in the woods."

"Pshaw, he has been stuffing you."

"Wasn't Mr. Ward stuffing you when he said there were wolves about?" I retorted. As my husband made no reply to this amiable rejoinder, I was able to enjoy my usual elation at having the last word.

"As long as this bear has probably eaten no one we may enjoy eating him, I suppose," said I presently.

"What makes you think this bear has eaten no one?" said Earl, who had been eating his share with great enjoyment.

"I think we would have heard of it if Bruin had been a cannibal, or at least Mr. Seymour would not have dared to send us any. Is not that sound reasoning, my boy?"

"Yes, I suppose so."

"How do you like bears, Lyle?" said his sister.

"Tell her that you like bear meat, but that you don't care for bears," said Allen.

As we rose from the table Doctor's Willie appeared at the door. "Meb is going to give Eddie Raymond a music lesson this afternoon," he said, "and would like to have you go with her, auntie."

"I will go if some one will keep house for me." Maidie consented to, as Allen had planned an excursion with Willie.

About two o'clock I started for the doctor's and found Meb about ready. We were soon on the way.

"I met Mrs. Raymond and Mrs. Racine just the day before Maidie came. We had a little chat at the boarding house, and I afterward saw them in the post office," said I. "I think Mrs. Racine was going away the next day."

"She went, I think, but Mr. Racine is here yet."

Crossing the railroad, we passed near the mill and walked on slowly, as the sun was warm, going over the same road that I had taken in my search for raspberries with Nora and the children for company. As we strolled along, flies buzzed about our faces, so we lazily swung branches to and fro, stopped to gather ferns, bright autumn leaves or a belated berry, talking of mutual friends who were far away or of new people we were learning to admire and like.

"Willie said you were going to give Eddie Raymond music lessons, Meb. I did not know you had become music teacher before."

"It *is* something new. I have Nora as pupil beside, but shall not give her a lesson to-day."

"Eddie is a little fellow, isn't he?"

"Yes, but a bright boy. His mother says he is always at the organ."

"Here is Mr. Thompson's house. He has gone to Hinckley to-day. I saw him as he started off."

"Did you hear of the trip 'the princess' made to Hinckley, with Mabel Nelson?"

"I heard they went. Did she enjoy it?"

"No, I don't think she did. Mabel had so many errands, they ran from store to store, and in fact were on the run about every moment, as they went on the eleven A. M. and came back about one P. M."

"They went up on the accommodation, I suppose."

"Yes, that is the only way."

"Have you been to Hinckley, Meb?"

"No, not yet, but I suppose mamma and I will go there and do some shopping before cold weather sets in."

"It is about as far as we were from the city, but

it will not be much like going into Minneapolis to shop, I imagine."

"No, not much; but they say Hinckley is a real enterprising town."

"I wish we could go there to church some Sunday. Doesn't it seem strange to spend Sunday as we do now?"

"It does seem an unusual way for us, but when the school house is completed we will at least have Sunday school. That will make it seem more like Sunday at the old home, to us all."

"Yes, it will to some of you, but as Lyle and Earl have whooping cough, I shall not like to take them this time of year, when other children will be exposed. I shall be glad to have the older children go, and their father will enjoy it."

"Here is Mrs. Anderson's house on the right," said Meb. "We have not a great deal farther to go." "Is Mrs. Raymond's the next house?" "No, Mrs. Molander lives in the next." "Is her house of logs?" "No, it is frame; they, as well as Mr. Anderson's people, are getting ready to lath and plaster, soon. Mrs. Molander's house is quite roomy." "She is Charlie Olson's sister," I said. "Another sister came lately and is visiting her. He was working for us the day she came, and asked leave to go to the train. We heard it stop, and came to the conclusion she had come."

"These houses will look very different inside when they are partitioned off, lathed and plastered," said Meb.

"Oh, yes, but they will seem cramped at first. After living in a large, open room, one does not get used at once to contracted walls. That expression reminds me of Winifred's contracting chamber in one of Mrs. Charles' works. Mrs. Charles is the author of 'The Schonberg Cotta Family,' a book you would enjoy, Meb. Winifred's brother, who was much older, told her a sort of allegory, in which she herself was the heroine. One day she found herself in a chamber, the walls of which seemed to contract at times, and at others to expand. When she was thinking of self alone, they closed in about her, but when her thoughts and interests went out to the wide world about her, the wonderful things it contained, and to the people who needed her help and sympathy, and love, she found her walls gradually expanding. Wasn't that a pretty conceit? I think we all get into contracting chambers occasionally, and we are apt to stay there too long."

"Yes," said Meb, "it is true."

"Here we are, and there is Mrs. Raymond at the door ready to welcome us."

"Good afternoon," said she, taking us into her pleasant little sitting room. "Sit down and rest.

Did the walk seem long to you?" addressing me. "Meb don't mind walking, I know."

"It did not seem at all long or tiresome," I replied. "Meb and I were so busy talking; but one usually finds a road longer the first time one goes over it."

"Then you have never been this way before?"

"I have never been so far as this on your road."

"Is Eddie ready for his lesson?" said Meb, after a few minutes talk.

"I will call him in," said his mother.

Then, as the little boy took his place at the organ, she said, "Come with me while I find some clean aprons for these little ones."

The two younger children were soon looking their best in clean suits and shining faces.

Meanwhile, Mrs. Raymond and I carried on a lively conversation, which was interrupted by the entrance of Mr. Racine, accompanied by another gentleman, whom he introduced, saying he was in our village for the purpose of organizing a Sabbath school.

"I hear you are intending to buy the boarding house and put in another store," I said to Mr. Racine.

"That is my business here, and my plans are about completed," he replied. "I shall go back soon to make arrangements about moving."

"I met your wife when she was here."

"She went away the day after we met you at the boarding house," said Mrs. Raymond, then turning to the other gentleman, said, "When do you expect to organize the school?"

"We are talking of having a meeting for that purpose in the boarding house to-morrow evening. I hope we will see you ladies there," and to Mrs. Raymond, "that you will furnish some scholars for our school."

"I shall try to be there," said she, "and intend to have my older children attend the school " was her reply.

"Have you called on many of the families here?" I asked.

"Not a great many," said he; "they are so scattered, but I have seen several and have sent word to others."

"I think you will have a fair number out."

"I hope so. Shall we see you?"

"It is doubtful, as we have a lonely walk and don't go away from home much after night sets in. I think my husband will be there unless something I do not know of prevents." Just then Meb came in, and after a little longer talk we rose to go.

"Will you not stay and take tea with me?" asked Mrs. Raymond.

"Not to-day. We thank you for the invitation, but as we are going to stop at Mrs. Anderson's and

Mrs. Molander's a few moments we can stay here no longer. You have quite a clearing about your house," I said to Mrs. Raymond as we went out. "I see you have potatoes here."

"Yes; we ploughed this up in the spring and planted potatoes. We do not want fires to creep up on us unawares."

Our stay at the other houses was short, as it was nearing five o'clock. I said to Charlie Olson's sisters, "I have seen quite a good deal of your brother. He is quiet, but we think him a thoroughly reliable and pleasant young man."

"Charlie is a good boy," said they. "We can always depend on him."

"When the Rush City party was here," said Meb, as we started homeward, "I went with one of the Mrs. Markhams to call on Mrs. Anderson, who was an old neighbor of hers."

"How did the ladies enjoy their stay here?"

"They were charmed, and said they were going to come and camp out next summer if possible."

"How did they come, on the train?"

"No, they came in carriages by way of Pine City."

"How many were there?"

"Four couples. The gentlemen had a great deal of business to see to."

"I supposed they would stay longer. They were only here over night, I think, were they not?"

"Yes, they started home the day after. They were at our house in the morning."

"I knew Mrs. Carver was expecting them. She told me that Mr. Carver had a telegram that they were coming."

"It must have taxed her to entertain so many. Her sleeping accommodations were not what she wished."

"Yes, but she is a wonderful woman; such a good cook and nice housekeeper, and so kind and even in her manner."

"I thought she had a real compliment one day when I was there. Frank and John had been out for a week or so, hard at work and roughing it. When they came back they seemed so pleased, and Frank said, 'There's no place like Mother Carver's home.'"

"You met quite a number of the settlers while you were at the boarding house, didn't you, auntie?"

"Yes, many more those first weeks than if I had gone immediately to housekeeping. Many that I met spoke to me, as I suppose they had heard who I was. I had to ask someone afterward who they were. I believe I did have a regular introduction to Mr. Seymour, Mr. Baty and Mr. Collier. They were all very cordial and pleasant to me. I think it must have been because we are 'Bound by the bonds of a common belief and a common misfortune.'"

"That line from 'Evangeline' always makes me think of a cousin of mine from Maine, a young lawyer who went out to Idaho when the country was new. He quoted that in one of his letters, in speaking of those he met there."

So Meb and I chatted as we journeyed on, and finally reached the parting of our ways, and went on homeward.

"Did you have a pleasant visit, mamma?" said Maidie, who had supper all ready.

"I had a very pleasant visit, and I think papa was right when he said that Mrs. Raymond's was a hospitable home."

"I am going some time with Meb. She likes to have company."

"I am sure you will enjoy it, and shall be glad to have you go some day soon."

CHAPTER V.

"GOOD BYE, MEB."

One morning we were at early breakfast when some one passed the window.

"Who can it be, so early?"

In a moment more Meb appeared at the door, fresh and sparkling with her morning walk.

Sitting down, she announced: "I have two budgets of news for you. One is, the box has come and is at our house; the other, Aunt May has invited me to come at once and spend a month with her."

"Splendid!" we cried. "Are you going, and how soon?"

"I am going to-morrow on the eleven, and mamma wants you to come right away and open the box."

"That'll be just fine for you, Cousin Meb, but how will auntie and 'the princess' get on without you?"

"'The princess,' dear, is as pleased as if it was herself who was to have the treat. She is going to help me get off and take my place when I am gone."

"She is a darling. Well, I think her turn will come."

"Must you go back?"

"Yes, at once. Can you come with me?"

"I think I will, and let Maidie take a trip later."

It was rather wet under foot that morning, as. it had rained some in the night. We picked our way through the "evergreen path" and turned into the short cut, reaching the house soon. As we approached, a pleasant picture appeared through the trees. A few stones had been piled up near the hammock, and a pleasant blaze kindled, while my sister reclined with her feet toward the fire, and "the princess" was flitting about, placing an easy chair for me near the "camp fire."

The girls opened the box, while I dried my shoes by the cheerful blaze. The box had been sent by a kind sister, to "save me a stitch or two." There were dresses, hats, jackets, cloaks, day wear and night wear, and magazines and picture papers for large and small. The garments were all nice, and there was something for each one.

Just then some one came up the path asking for the doctor. I turned, and was introduced to Mr. Jay Braman.

"Like ships meeting at sea and passing, never again to signal each other," was my thought afterward when I recalled that brief meeting.

"We are so nicely off now for winter clothing," I said to my sister. "I have a large box packed full of flannel underwear and we have cloaks, dresses and coats for every one of the seven. In fact, I cannot think of anything we shall need for cold weather except a new suit for Allen and stockings and mittens for the children. Their father has two good suits he has hardly worn, he has been doing such rough work this season. I wish every family of our size were as well fixed for winter as we are."

"You are fortunate indeed," she replied. "It has been such hard times, I am afraid many families will be in need of warm clothing as well as daily bread this winter."

Teams were scarce and the men's time valuable, so "the princess" and I loaded our arms and started through the woods, I sending back as we disappeared, a kiss with "Good bye" to Meb, who stood near her mother, the firelight kindling roses in her cheeks. Maidie made a trip back and returned about noon, saying, "Meb has gone, 'the princess' and I went to see her off."

After dinner I said to my little boys, "Would you like to take a walk with mamma?"

"Oh, yes."

"Shall we go and see the ding dong?" asked Lyle anxiously.

"Yes, we will wait till four o'clock if you want to see the train. Now run and play with your little carts." With reading and sewing the time quickly passed and a little before four we started toward the "city" as I called it. Going into the post office we found that we had yet a few minutes to wait before the 4:20 train would appear.

"With your permission, Mr. Berg, I will try your hammock while I am waiting."

"Certainly," he said.

The hammock was suspended under the trees at some distance from the house, as there were no trees very near. It was between the boarding house and Mr. Berg's store. As the children and I were seated there swinging to and fro Mrs. Berg came out to the trees, and rising, I talked with her for some time.

"Are you getting settled?" she inquired kindly.

"Yes, to some extent. I am ready to see my friends."

"I shall try and come soon, though with my three little ones it is hard to get away from home."

"We have been so busy getting our house in shape that my work has been doubled."

"It must have been, but you are nearly through now, are you not?"

"Yes, we are just about through."

"How are you going to like it here?" she continued.

"It seems wild and lonely, but I suppose I shall like it better the longer I stay. It is my home now."

"I wonder if the people who look out of the car windows do not pity us as they go by," she said, as the train came steaming up and passed us.

"I don't know; perhaps they do not give us a thought." Seeing Mrs. Carver and a younger lady approaching I said, "I suppose that is young Mrs. Carver with her mother. I heard she arrived a few days ago."

"Yes, she has the little boys with her."

As they approached, the elder lady, seeing us under the trees, stopped and spoke to us, introducing her daughter. After a few minutes' talk they went on to the office, while I continued my conversation with Mrs. Berg, learning that she was a normal graduate, had been a teacher for years before her marriage, and even with her strong taste for good reading could hardly reconcile herself to the lack of society she found in this new place. Soon after, Lyle and Earl having seen the "ding dong," we went back, and as we passed near the boarding house, again met young Mrs. Carver and stopped for a little chat. Her stay was to be brief, but she accepted my invitation to come and call with her mother, and bidding her good bye I went on toward home.

I had promised the doctor to make a collection of leaves for him to exhibit at the state fair. Thinking of this promise I set to work to gather those that were within reach.

"Ah, here are Maidie and 'the princess.' Now I will have some help."

"What are you doing," asked the girls as they approached.

"I am making a beginning," said I, "and would like some help." Then noticing their puzzled looks I continued. "I am going to try and make a collection of different leaves for the doctor. See, I have already maple, basswood, poplar, spruce, fir, pine and cherry."

"You had better come over by our house and you will find some you have not already collected, auntie," said "the princess."

"I will go for a few moments, as I have not seen your mother this week." The girls were soon gathering leaves for me, while I talked with my sister in the house.

"Why do you call cousin 'the princess?'" said matter-of-fact Earl one day.

"Because she is a daughter of the King," said I, looking down into his earnest eyes.

"Is she; how do you know, mamma?"

"I know because she is kind and unselfish and loves to obey the King," I replied. "Is not that a sure sign?"

"Yes, mamma," said the boy, as he ran off to play.

The nights were growing cooler, though at times it was still hot at mid-day. "We will soon ask you to lay the upper floor," said I to my husband; "the

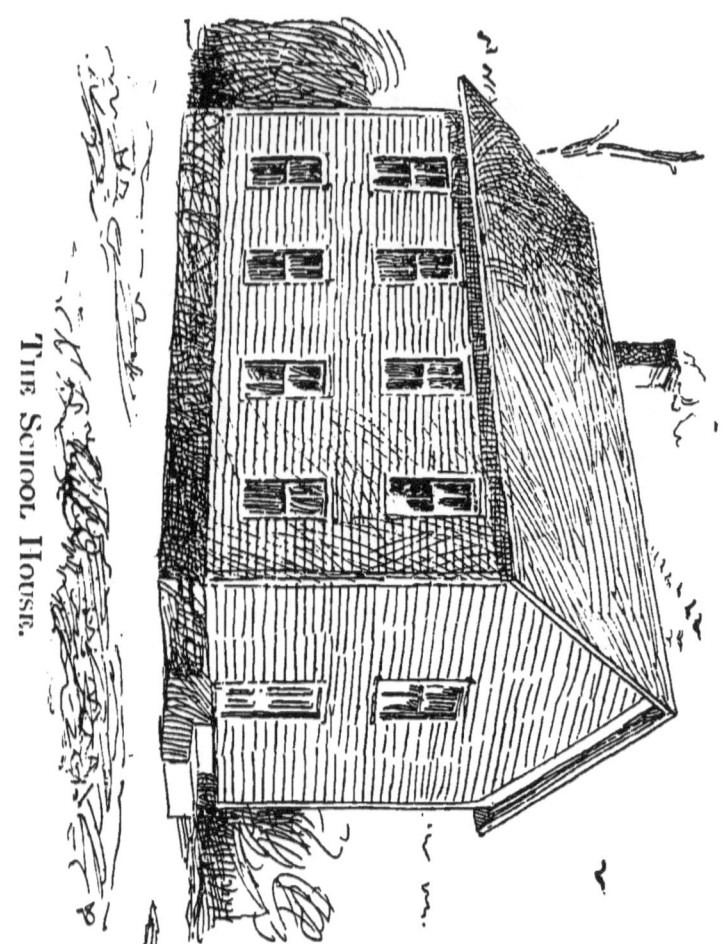

The School House.

cracks in this single floor will let in a great deal of cold before long."

"Yes, it must be done soon, but our work is nearly finished on the school house. Then I shall have plenty to do at home for a while. The doctor will want me to help on his house soon. When a a few of these important things are done, our house will be comfortable for cold weather."

CHAPTER VI.

PREMONITIONS.

"This is the first day of September" said I, at the breakfast table. "We will be sure to have frost before very long. I am glad I have my chrysanthemums safely housed."

"I think there will be a great many blossoms on them, mamma," said Maidie. "What did you do with Flo's bush?"

"I put her's with mine. They look very thrifty, and I discovered some buds on them yesterday."

"Come Allen," said his father, as we arose from the table, "we will go down to the dam below the potato field and get out some boards. They will be of great use to me when I am ready to build my barn."

Our morning passed quickly, as Maidie and I were busy with our usual Saturday's work.

"Dinner is ready," said the little cook "and it is after twelve. I wonder why papa and Allen do not come?"

We had noticed all the morning that the smoke away southeast was quite dense, and the wind had been growing stronger. Several times as we worked, we had remarked on the danger of fire spreading unusually in such a wind.

"Perhaps they have gone to help fight fire. The smoke seems to be in that direction."

"I am sure some one is in danger, mamma, the wind is so strong and the smoke spreads over the sky more than I ever saw it before."

"You had better run down to the meadow through 'the arched road' and see if they are coming," said I, as the minutes passed and still they did not appear. "I will put this bread in the baking tins while you are gone. We will keep up the fire and finish our Saturday baking as soon as we can. It is growing oppressively warm."

Maidie rushed away, but soon came back, saying she could see no signs of them.

"We will eat our dinner then, as the little ones are hungry, and keep the dinner warm for the others. How did the smoke seem down there?" said I, as we sat at the table, leisurely eating.

"It seems to be getting worse all the while, mamma. What if it should come this way?"

"I will go down after I am through and see what I think of it. The wind does blow harder than it did before noon, I am sure. I am afraid there is trouble somewhere."

"Let me go with you," pleaded Maidie, as I put on my hat and started for the meadow.

"The little boys will not like to be left alone," said I, with some hesitation.

"You'll stay and take care of Lyle, won't you Earl?" she said coaxingly

"Yes, I'll stay," said he.

We had now begun to feel a vague restlessness, unusual to us both, and hurried through the winding path which led over many obstacles, and finally dropped down several feet at the edge of the meadow, where the branches drooped so low that we had to stoop as we passed beneath. As we emerged into the open meadow we could see the smoke rolling toward the north, far to the southeast.

"It is farther away than it seems, but it is a dreadful fire, I think. If it should come up as far as this, I think it will go a good deal to the east of us, and may take some of those grand elms papa is so proud of. I hate to think of having any of those fine trees burned. There are so many beautiful ones on the other side of the creek. If the fire does come through to-day we are helpless to save them."

"I do wish papa would come," said Maidie, "I will climb this high stack and perhaps I will see him."

In a few moments she slid down saying, "I can see no one coming."

"We must go back to the children now," said I, turning homeward.

"How hot it is getting!" complained Maidie, taking off her hat.

"The sun is extremely hot and the wind is like

the scorching south winds we used to have in Dakota at times, regular simooms they seemed."

We found the little ones contentedly playing about. The wind was blowing into the south and west windows, and though the fire in the cook stove had gone out, the room was uncomfortably warm.

"See the bread, mamma," said Maidie.

It had risen high and was beginning to run over, but feeling incapable of settling to anything just then, I kneaded it down, thinking that when my husband and Allen returned, I would start up the fire and put it in the oven. "I feel anxious about papa and Allen," I said at length, "and I must see how the fire is, down that way."

"Let us take the children and go down again," said their sister, after we had vainly striven to quiet down and continue the usual Saturday work.

Putting on their hats we locked the doors and again hurried through the thicket, half carrying the children, and urging them along in our increasing excitement. Again, after we reached a point where we had a long view down the meadow, Maidie climbed a stack to get a better view in that direction.

"They are coming," she called. "Papa and Allen are coming and they are walking very slowly. Oh, see how the smoke pours over this way and how black it is!"

The fact that they at last were coming and that

they were coming slowly, reassured me, and we
started on with the little boys, knowing that they
would soon overtake us. As they approached I
asked, "Why were you so long? It must be nearly
two o'clock."

"We got out about twenty dollars worth of lumber and then put it into the water for fear it would
be burned."

"So the fire had not reached as far as there when
you left?"

"No, but there is great danger; the wind is terrible."

"Are you not tired out and hungry?" as we hurried to the house.

"Yes, very tired and hungry," but I could see
that the same premonitory feeling of danger affected
my husband, and he and the boy ate very little.

Maidie began to wander round in a distracted
way. I took a little basket, used as a lunch basket,
and going to the bureau took out my gold watch,
pocket book, my glasses, new and carefully fitted to
my eyes a few weeks before in the city, looked for
some valuable papers, and put in some clean pocket
handkerchiefs. As I did not find the papers I was
looking for at once, I turned to Maidie saying, "If
the fire comes this way we must have some of the
children's clothes bundled up." Telling her what to
select, I succeeded in getting her to gather together

and tie into a bundle, two good suits for the little
boys and a dress for herself.

"You had better put down the windows," said my
husband, as the wind was tearing through the house,
blowing draperies and shades in a frantic way and
threatening to break the slender plants in the window boxes.

"Where are you going?" said he, as I hung the
basket on my arm and put on my hat.

"I am going to see if there will be any chance for
us to escape through 'the evergreen path' or through
the meadow to the doctor's, if the fire comes toward
the house."

"Don't go," he said. "You had better stay here."

"I must. I will turn back if I see I am in any
danger." So saying I started off alone. Through
our wood road the air was quite clear and I was un-
troubled by smoke, though it seemed as if the smoke
was coming that way, which surprised me, as I was
then going toward the west. I thought "There
must be another fire. This surely is not the same
one we have been watching." Turning into "the
evergreen path" I hurried toward the school house.
But when I came to the place, about half way through,
where the trees were so dense, I began to realize
that the smoke was filling these woods. As I turned
to go back, I saw a squirrel run back and forth as if
uncertain which way to go, and noticed that the air
was strangely still and that leaves were dropping

noiselessly. Hurrying back I met Allen at the entrance to the path.

"Papa sent me for you," said he.

"We will hurry back," said I, saying little to my boy on the way, not wishing to rouse his fears for our safety. As I reached the house my husband was busy doing something about the west side, what, I knew not at the time, though later learned that he was pouring water on a pile of chips and lumber near by, and had been up on the house pulling boards from the roof.

He said, shortly, "You should not have gone away."

"I am satisfied now," I returned, quietly, "that it would be of no use for us to try and escape that way. If we cannot save ourselves here we are lost."

Going round to the east door I went in, my husband saying, "I will go down to the meadow and see how it looks," disappearing immediately through the short cut.

Maidie had been vainly trying to put the kitten into a bag and keep her in while she tied it up. Finally, giving up in despair, she turned to me with a helpless look on her face. I put the little basket on my sewing machine, and realizing at last that the fire was almost on us, though I did not then glance towards the woods, I said to Maidie, "Bring some blankets and come out to the well." Snatching one

from the bed myself, Maidie followed with another.
A tub full of water stood near the well. I immersed the blankets in this water, and with my
daughter's help dashed two or three pails of water
on the wooden platform over the well.

"Quick, the ladder! Come Maidie, come Allen."
Dashing into the house we three dragged out the
heavy ladder, got it down into the well, and I began
to tie on two pails each side, on the rounds I could
reach from the top.

Earl had begun to cry in his fright and bewilderment, and I tried to reassure him saying, "We will
be all right; the fire will not harm us."

"Papa, papa," called Maidie, who at the last moment began to regain her presence of mind, "come
back, quick." Running into the house she snatched
a light spread from the bed, just as her father returned, and running to the well he sprung down the
ladder with the tub and a little box just at hand.

Rabbits were flocking about the well, running
back and forth in sudden bewilderment. I do not
remember to have seen any other living creature.
The kitten had some time before vanished in the
woods beyond the house.

CHAPTER VII.

THE FIRE IS COMING.

We were now all close by, except Maidie. Her papa turned the tub bottom side up in the water, forcing it down so it rested on the bottom, and placing the box on it, he was up in a flash. Maidie appeared at the door with the quilt in her hand. Calling to her to close the door, he caught hold of Earl's arm; meantime Maidie and Allen scrambled down the ladder. Forcing the struggling and screaming little boy down after them, his father waited a moment till I followed with little Lyle, then he stepped down after us just far enough for his head to come under the platform, exclaiming "Oh, the poor little rabbits!"

With a rush, and a roar, and a fearful glare of light, the fire was upon us in intense fury. One glance upward showed me this, then I turned to the children.

Allen clung to the ladder, then stepped down on the tub, on which, and the box, stood Maidie, Earl and Lyle, huddled closely together. I had stepped down into the water, which was only knee deep.

Maidie's quilt had been dropped into the water, and this we spread dripping wet over our heads, so that the five of us who stood below, were for the

present protected from chance sparks and fiery
brands. My husband spread one of the wet
blankets that had been placed in the tub, over his
head, under the square opening through which the
ladder projected.

"Oh," he groaned, "if I had only got the ladder
out, we might have closed the opening."

"But how could we ever get out," said I, "if you
had done that?"

After a time, realizing that I was standing in the
water, he exclaimed, "You must not stand there!"

Untying one of the pails, which I had suspended
by ropes, thinking the little boys might stand in
them out of water, he turned it upside down in the
water, put a thick board which happened to be
floating in the well, on top of the pail, and with one
foot on the pail and the other on the tub, which was
close by, I kept out of the water.

Earl and Lyle kept crying incessantly, as well as
coughing and strangling. Allen kept perfectly
quiet, but Maidie began to spin around as if she
was dizzy.

The sparks, ashes and cinders dropped in showers
about us, but we shook them off, and kept wetting
the tops of our heads, faces and lips in the water,
putting it to the children's mouths, in spite of their
cries, dashing it also on their heads at intervals.

"Don't cry, Earl, God will take care of us.
Keep still, Lyle, that's a good boy." I kept repeat-

ing. "What is the matter, Maidie? Don't faint, you'll fall into the water for I can't hold you. Keep your head cool; Papa, untie the other pail; Allen, dip it into the water and hand it up for her to drink."

Calm and forgetful of self, my husband stood above, keeping the wet blanket well over us and from his nearness to the opening at the top, getting some idea of the progress of the fire.

With the spread dragging heavily on head and shoulders, I kept trying to quiet and reassure the frightened children. The heat was now intense and the smoke began to be more thick and suffocating.

"We cannot stand this long" I thought, but before our endurance gave out, the smoke cleared to some extent, and we began to breathe more freely.

From crying, Earl began to talk incoherently and in little gasps repeated, "God will take care,—We'll go to hebben, won't we?—God will take us to hebben,—He won't let us suf— The fire won't hurt," keeping it up so long, that I began to fear the child was getting flighty.

"Oh," said papa, from above, "the house is on fire; oh, this is terrible, we must pray to God to save us."

From our hearts the prayer ascended, though our lips could frame no words.

Still the children cried piteously, while Maidie moaned, "Oh, my head, my head!" Still we shook off burning sparks, and held the water, now full of burnt cinders and ashes, to our mouths. Our lips and tongues were dry, our throats parched with heat, and constantly we wet the covering over our heads.

Maidie revived a little, and called, "Oh, papa, is not the worst over?"

Hesitatingly he replied, "I am afraid not."

"Is the house burning yet?"

"Oh, yes, but happily the wind takes the flames past us."

"How fortunate the well is in this direction and no nearer the house!"

To quiet the little ones I said, "Let us sing, 'Jesus loves me.'" The two older children joined with me, and we sang softly,

> "Jesus loves me, he who died,
> Heaven's gate to open wide;
> He will wash away my sin,
> Let his little child come in."

Gradually the sobs died away, and the little ones were brave and quiet the remainder of the time.

Still the roar of the fire sounded in our ears, and scorching heat waves beat upon our heads. From leaning against the damp earth at the side of the well to steady myself, I began to feel cold chills creeping over me, though my head seemed bursting with the heat. Earl also complained of being chilly. My husband's arm began to cramp, but he had made no complaint before.

"Is not the heat abating," I asked anxiously. "I think it is a little," he answered, to my great relief.

"Just as soon as we can endure having our heads above ground, we must get out," I replied, "for we will get chilled and suffer in consequence.

After a little he said, "I think we can venture out now."

One by one we emerged from the well, and oh, the desolation of the sight spread out before our eyes! A blackened, dreary waste as far as eye could see. Not a timber left of the house, only a gaping, smoking cellar.

All the beautiful trees laid low, only the dark trunks left; all smoking, many still burning. Nothing green in all the world, and waves of scorching heat rising all about us as we stood bareheaded and soiled and panting by the ruins of our home.

Drawing off baby's shoes and stockings I set his shoes on a log, and spread out his stockings to dry, spreading out my own skirts also, that the hot air might pass through them.

Near the well lay an axe and hammer, whose handles were not greatly injured. Going over to where the house had stood and looking down into the cellar, we saw scattered parts of the sewing machine, remnants of the stove and a few broken dishes. All else had been consumed in the fierce, melt-in   heat

Homeless, desolate and forlorn, where should we turn!

"Oh, I am afraid the doctor's people are burned," said Maidie. "Their well was so near the house they could not have gone in there, I am sure."

"We must start and see, and not delay," said my husband.

"Can we not stay a little while and dry ourselves? It will not take long."

"No; night is coming on. We must try and find a place of shelter."

Putting on Lyle's shoes and taking his stockings in my hand, papa and Allen with each a wet blanket, and the rest following, we started on. As we crossed into the meadow, papa came back and taking up little Earl, who was barefooted, carried him over the burning ground.

"Oh, oh," screamed Maidie, who followed, "I am burning my feet." As I sprang over the hot ashes and roots with little Lyle in my arms, hot coals stuck to my shoes, but in a few moments we were in the meadow where, though it was dry and crisp under foot, we could endure the heat of the ground.

On we went, crossing the creek and hurrying over the crisped grass, keeping well away from the trees, up whose bare trunks fire was running, while at intervals they fell about us in distances more or less remote.

A forlorn company was this, silhouetted against

the dark background of blackened ground and stump and tree, all pride of appearance, apparel and condition swallowed up in the one thought of anxiety for the dear ones we might never see alive, the one desire, a shelter for the night, a place to rest our weary heads.

My own head was in the condition known to all who suffer from nervous sick headaches, and fast becoming worse.

I began to realize how my husband was suffering as at intervals he dropped on his knees and put his hands over his eyes, then he would rise and go on, seemingly forgetful of us all, even the little barefooted boy who trudged uncomplainingly at his side.

At last we reached the Doctor's potato field, and looking towards where the tree embowered house had stood, no vestige of it appeared. All was blank desolation and ruin. "Oh, where can they be?" thought I, with a sinking heart.

"Let us pull up a hill of potatoes and see if they are burned," said Allen.

"No," said his papa, "do not delay," but as I passed through the field, I grasped a plant and pulling it up, found the potatoes sound and unscorched.

On we went, crossing soon, prostrate telegraph wires, stepping over smoking railroad ties, and rails that might be burning hot, and turning, walked on to where Mr. Nelson's house had stood.

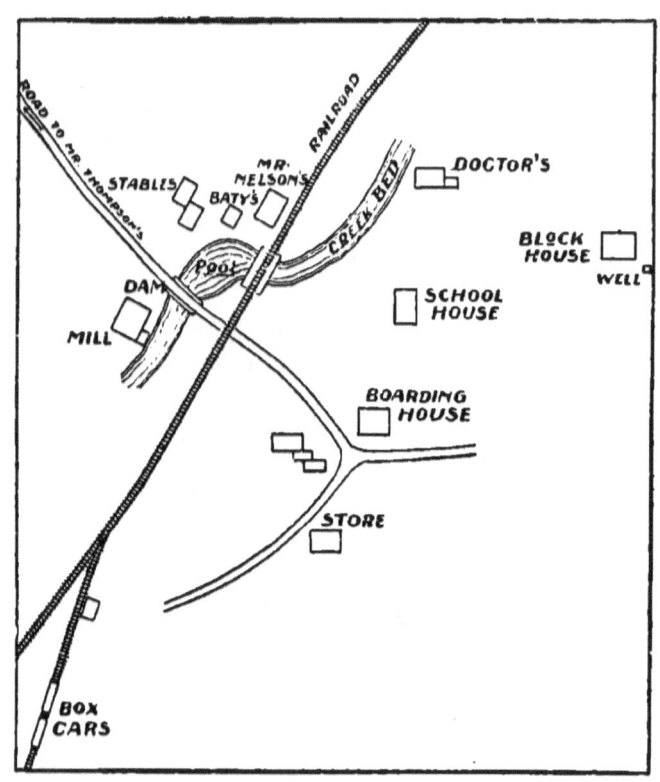

MAP OF SETTLEMENT.

The first sound we heard in all the wide, desolate expanse, was a cow bell.

Passing the smoking ruins of Mr. Nelson's house, and those of Mr. Baty's near by, we stood on the bank above the pool, and looking down saw such a sight as I hope never to see again.

Grouped upon the bank of the pool were our friends and neighbors, in attitudes betokening despair, suffering and hopeless misery. We recognized first the Doctor's wife and three children, Maidie exclaiming, "Oh, there they are!" with a tone of intense relief.

Mr. Baty, partially blindfolded, came forward and assisted me down the bank, while my husband helped the children.

"Oh, my dear sister," I exclaimed, "you do not know how relieved I feel to find you safe. But where is Doctor?" I said presently, failing to see him among the people about me.

"We do not know. Mr. Collier and Mr. Gonyea think he was overpowered in the fire."

"Surely you do not think so."

"No, I believe he will soon be with us."

Most of the group were so covered or blindfolded, that it was only by slow degrees that we recognized them, or learned from my sister and others near by, who they were.

With backs to a trunk dragged from Mr Baty's house, and unscorched by the fire, sat Mrs. Carver and Mrs. Baty, completely enveloped by a quilt. Willie was stretched full length on the ground with face downward by his mother's side, while Carlton sat near, with his hat over his eyes, enduring with patient fortitude the smarting, burning sensation in those delicate organs. A little beyond sat Mrs. Berg, enveloped also by a quilt, with her baby half undressed in her lap, and her dear little girls near her, all in an attitude mutely expressing intense misery and suffering.

Here was a man stretched full length on the ground, so covered as to be unrecognizable, whom I afterward learned was Mr. Gonyea, hands and feet terribly burned, as well as eyes and lungs aching from smoke and heat combined.

Mr. Berg was quietly ministering to his little family, while Willie Berg lay stretched on the ground.

Mrs. Nelson and her two youngest children formed another pathetic group, while Mr. Seymour, a little farther away, was suffering much as my husband, who now dropped on the ground, adding another figure to the sorrowful group.

All were quiet and patient. No one groaned, none of the children cried, but the calm endurance of all but added to the terrible pathos of the scene. Calling Maidie to hold my head, I stepped to one side and obtained relief to some extent from the racking headache I had been suffering from since leaving the well. A second vomiting spell an hour or so later completed the cure. Many others, especially among the children, found relief in this way soon after the fire, though poor little Minnie Nelson suffered with the terrible sickness for a much longer time.

Another party joined us, and as they approached a sweet little voice chanted, "All yi, all yi." Dear little Vernon was in his grandma's arms, and she told us that he had gone through it all quietly without an outcry.

There were other groups a little farther away, whom we could only dimly see, as the smoke was so suffocating and blinding, and night was fast coming on.

Some one brought potatoes for us to roast for our supper, others tore up aprons and passed the strips to those who needed bandages for their eyes, which included nearly every one.

"Friends, we are all on a level now," said Mr. Ward, but presently demonstrated that he was not quite on a level with some in suffering or in apathy, by starting off to reconnoiter for shelter during the night. He presently brought us word that he had discovered some box cars on the track toward Mora. It was fast growing dark, and bidding the children each take a potato, I, with my family, my sister and her children, and others started down the track in our quest for shelter.

Over burning ties and smoking ground we walked

nearly a mile, reaching at last two box cars, which
had been switched off to the side track.   One contained bundles of lath, the other, brick; all for the
doctor's house.   With the help of the men, women
and children were soon within the first car.

The laths were piled in tiers at one side of the
car, one quite high, close to the end, where a square
opening let in air; the other tier was lower down.
The floor was clear on the other side of the car.

There were then only Mr. and Mrs. Ward and
their son in the car, besides my family and the
doctor's, numbering thirteen in all.

"Where are the others?" I asked.   "I supposed
they were coming too."

We learned soon afterwards that they started up
the railroad toward Hinckley, were met there by a
train whose engine was turned from the track by
spreading rails, and spent the night as we did, in
stationary cars.

This party afterwards went on to Pine City, and
we saw them no more.

We did not know until the next morning, of the
terrible holocaust at Hinckley, and then only meager
reports, which we were hardly able to credit.

We disposed ourselves on the bundles of laths,
some sitting and some lying down, making ourselves
as comfortable as possible under the circumstances.
Soon after, a party of about thirty Jews came up
to the car.   They had also saved themselves as we

learned the others had done, by keeping under water to their necks, and constantly dipping their heads in. But for the smoke and our dim eyes, we would have seen them before, huddled together near the others.

We tried to persuade them to go into the other car, that all might not be so crowded, but finally yielded to their wishes, and allowed them to climb in where we were.

As the night came on, dense darkness settled down, relieved only by the fitful light from burning lumber near us, and stumps and trees still on fire across the track.

The scene within that crowded car would have touched the hardest heart. About forty men, women and children lay stretched on the rough laths, sitting, with weary heads against the sides of the car, or lying at full length upon the floor, so closely packed together that it was impossible to move about without the utmost care.

Some of the mothers forgot their little ones, who bravely accepted the situation and dropped off to sleep without pillow or coverlet. Others groaned and caught brief snatches of sleep, wakened by their cramped state of discomfort, to long wakeful hours of misery.

All this time the doctor's wife knew not whether her husband would ever come to her again. Bravely her wifely heart kept up hope, refusing to believe him among the dead. About ten in the evening, the sound of the doctor's voice was heard outside the car.

The princess almost shouted with glee, while Carlton and Willie, who had been dozing, wakened and joined in the general rejoicing. The relief of my sister was very evident, though she was so quiet. If I had not been in much the same state myself, I should have wondered then at her apparent apathy at that time, and also before she knew that her almost idolized husband was indeed safe. Afterward, I realized that the strain of such imminent danger for a time seemed to paralyze our faculties, and that for a long while none of us could think beyond the present moment, or comprehend anything clearly outside of our own unusual and still precarious situation.

"Oh, uncle," said Maidie, "they told us such dreadful things about you."

"How could you have got through when Mr. Gonyea was so badly burned?" I asked.

"It is a story I will tell you at another time," he replied.

"Not one of our number is missing," said my husband, who had roused himself for a moment.

We heard nothing then of any burns, as doctor gave us merely a brief statement of his desperate fight with the fire in company with Big Joe, whom he led by the hand. In the morning we discovered that his eyes were swollen and blinded, and great blisters stood up on the back of his hand.

Hearing that Mr. Gonyea, by his own request, had been left by those who had gone on towards Hinckley, the doctor, led by men who had some use of their eyes, went up the track to see if anything could be done for the poor man before settling down for the night. He came back with the news that Mr. Gonyea desired to remain where he was, and that a train from Hinckley would come to our relief in the morning.

With this hope to cheer us we settled down as best we could to endure the long hours of the night.

CHAPTER VIII.

ONE SUNDAY'S EXPERIENCES.

At intervals those who slept would rouse and words would be exchanged.

"Oh, is it not nearly morning?" called one wearily. Mr. Ward struck a match and looked at his watch. It was nearly two o'clock. I think we were all glad that it was after midnight. "The sun rises at 5:29. We will see the morning light before many hours," was the cheering word of one.

At one time, feeling oppressed by the atmosphere within the car, I left my little sleepers' heads in care of "the princess," who was at my side, and carefully stepping around the prostrate forms of sleepers on the floor, reached the wide entrance, and standing there inhaled breaths of purer, though smoke-laden air.

Before me rose a city brilliantly illuminated; some lights low down in basements, others higher; still others in lofty stories; while little points, like electric lights, shone through the seemingly misty air. Over all the silent stars shone with softly tempered radiance.

So like lights in city windows, gleaming from afar, seemed those rays from burning tree and stump, and leafless trunk, that I returned to my weary vigil not a little comforted by the weird imagination.

In the early evening, we had discovered that the ties were on fire under our car. Feeling uneasy, my now blind husband went outside, and after a time, with the help of a better pair of eyes, succeeded in extinguishing it.

As the night wore on, the doctor's wife, enveloped in a blanket, yet shivering with cold, as her wet clothing still clung to her, began to suffer with an old trouble which threatened to take away her breath entirely. The doctor and "the princess" chafed her hands, and worked over her until she was relieved, but at intervals these spells returned to add to her discomfort and suffering, already hard to endure.

The brave little "princess," herself grew more hoarse, and distressing coughing spells disturbed her already broken rest.

Mrs. Ward, who was suffering with her eyes, as well as my husband, endured patiently and silently. Her boy, who was very sick the first part of the night, found some relief and rest in forgetful slumber. The little Jewish children endured with wonderful patience their share of the general discomfort, taking the unusual circumstances in a matter of fact way, and making no complaint.

At last, morning came to cheer us with the prospects of speedy relief. Water was brought to us, a pail full at a time, and so great was the demand for it by our thirsty and smoke-dried throats, that we found it very difficult to keep a few drops to bathe hands and faces, or to wet the indispensable bandages on our eyes. Potatoes were scraped and used as poultices to relieve the pain and smart in our eyes.

"Mamma," said Allen from outside the car, "we have found some eggs that were dropped from the train yesterday for Mr. Berg. They are cooked by the fire and every one can have hard baked eggs for breakfast."

As we had had nothing to eat since the noon before, the brown shells were soon removed, and these eggs with potatoes and raw cabbage constituted a breakfast not to be despised.

"We ought to be thankful," said patient Carlton, who sat as the night before, with hat drawn over his eyes, "that we have any breakfast at all."

"Indeed, we should," was the hearty reply.

Some of us felt the lack of combs, handkerchiefs, and water enough to bathe faces and hands freely more than anything else, but when after dark on that Sunday night I at last obtained a comb it would not go through my hair, which was matted with ashes, dust and cinders.

We heard no word of complaint from the doctor, but exhausted with pain and fatigue he kept very quiet the first part of the day. Once he said, "Some

After the Fire.

one ought to go and see if Mr. Gonyea needs anything."

No one else volunteered, and believing myself to
be as able-bodied as any one there, and much more
so than some, I made up my mind to at least walk
up to where he had been left, and try and encourage
him. Climbing down from the car I began my walk
along the track. No fear of heavy freight trains
now, or of the Limited dashing through with tre-
mendous speed.

The ground was still smoking in so many places
that it was impossible for me to uncover my eyes
with any comfort, so spreading one thickness of
cloth over them, I walked on, avoiding carefully the
many pitfalls by the way, going round a dangerous
place I remembered passing by the night before.

When opposite our settlement I found it impossible to locate any house in that direction. At last,
as I neared the ruined trestle, I saw what I knew
must be the ruins of the mill, smoking and blazing
as well. Further on a pile of sawdust was sending
up a dismal volume of smoke, and taking my bear-
ings by these, I crossed over and passed on in the
vicinity where the stables had stood. A great ox
lay turned on one side, and as the creature seemed
not to be burned, even slightly, I concluded that it
had been suffocated.

Of the many who the day before had been
burned to death, we were spared the sight.

Going on a little further, I passed near where
Mr. Baty's house had stood. As I before men-
tioned, it was a very small frame building and I
suppose burned so quickly as not to injure Mrs.
Baty's trunk, which still remained on the bank
below. I noticed then the ruins of their stove, and
a pail near by, in which there were several articles
for household use. Turning about, I almost stum-
bled against a large easy chair, which was burned
but little, though the seat was partly gone.

Looking down over the bank towards the place
where we had seen the people in desolate groups
the night before, the solitary figure there was Mr.
Gonyea, completely covered with quilts, motionless
and voiceless. I was soon at his side, and asked,
after bidding him "Good morning," "Is there anything I can do for you?"

"I think not," said he, "unless you can find something for me to eat. I have had nothing since yesterday morning."

"I am quite sure I can," I replied, amazed at his
brave endurance of pain, hunger and exposure.

In the pail by Mr. Baty's house, I found crackers
and biscuits, and leaving some potatoes to roast in
the burning roots of an old stump, with the help
of Frank, who soon after appeared, I presently fed
him with the bread and roast potatoes, and gave
him as good water as we could find, bound his poor
hands and feet with scraped potatoes, and reluctantly

leaving him still covered with quilts sodden with water, went back to the car. The sorrowful sight of his hands and feet, blackened and blistered, with skin peeling off, helped me to realize the suffering I and my dear ones had been spared.

Among the discomforts of that morning sojourn in the dingy, uncomfortable car, the joy of seeing one and another come up, whom we feared might be burned to death, stood out in strong relief. Rumors came at intervals of bodies being found near the track disfigured beyond recognition. As we thought of one after another of our neighbors of whose welfare we knew not, our hearts filled with grave misgivings.

Where are Frank and John, and Mr. Thompson and Mr. Raymond's people? Where are Jay Braman, Mr. Anderson and family, Mr. Molander and his family? Where is Charlie Olson? Where Mr. Frame's people, and what of Mrs. Braman? while other names with whom I was less familiar, were spoken.

Before I started up the track to look after Mr. Gonyea, some of the burden was lifted from our hearts by the appearance of Frank and John, Mr. Thompson, Mrs. Frame and part of her family, and Mrs. Braman. Jakey also had joined us.

As we passed down the track the night before we had met Alice and Mabel Nelson, with some of the young section hands, coming back from their trip after cranberries that day, but in fair condition, having found shelter and help in their time of peril.

Mrs. Frame and her boys, with Mrs. Braman, had started for cranberries the day before, fortunately taking plenty of water with them. When the fire rushed upon them, they took refuge under an over-hanging bank of the creek, eaten out by the thicket. Saturating their clothes with water, and sheltered by an alder thicket, they came through all right, though suffering much from exposure during the following night.

When they appeared at the box car the following morning, we were glad to share with them what comforts we had to offer.

Mrs. Braman had then seen neither husband or son, and though we assured her that Mr. Braman was safe, having been in the water with those who took refuge near the mill, and heroically helped to sustain women and children in their dangerous positions, yet she felt sure that her son had suffered death, and that she would see his face no more.

Poor, tearful, heart-broken mother, her fears were too well grounded!

Vainly we tried to comfort her, and bade her hope, feeling in our hearts even before we knew with certainty, that hopes were vain.

Mrs. Frame knew not whether her husband was safe, but he soon appeared, having safely passed through the fire, as well as Dave, the oldest son.

Now indeed we were "Bound by the bonds of a common belief and a common misfortune," rejoicing with a common joy, sorrowing with a common sorrow. All were friends and brothers and sisters.

Poor Mr. Barnes, he too mourned a son. Coming into the car about noon, the old gentleman, who had been "baching it" with his son, went up to the doctor and said in trembling tones, as tears gathered in his eyes, "I fear the worst for my poor boy." [They had not been together the day of the fire.] Patiently and sorrowfully, he sat with us, and our hearts went out with deep sympathy to him. Later, his two daughters from St. Panl came into the car, and their quiet sorrow touched all hearts.

During the day, word was brought that Mrs. Molander, her sister and two children had been found just outside at the corner of her house, burned and disfigured, but no word came of the families near her.

At last relief came to us, for those outside announced a hand-car from Mora. A moment more, and it stopped on the main track opposite our car, crowded with men who said, "Aren't you glad to see somebody?"

"Indeed, we are," was the answer.

These kind friends handed up dinner pails containing bread, meat and other substantial articles of food, and left us, saying that they would come back again with more supplies and a chance for some of

us to go back with them. They soon repassed us
with Mr. Gonyea and Jakey, en route for Mora,
where our brave sufferer was kindly cared for, and
his wounds properly dressed.

We were then still crowded in one car, and the
eatables were divided among all, there being enough
to satisfy us at that time and some to spare, for I
saw one Jewish woman, after we were through
eating, carefully guarding a lap full of bread and
meat. Her wisdom in providing for future needs
was certainly commendable.

Soon after this some of us concluded to try the
other car, and by piling bricks for seats and beds
and pillows, and sweeping the floor with the side of
a lath, we had a cleaner and hence more comfortable place, into which the doctor's family, Mrs.
Frame's, Mr. Ward's and my own with Mr. Barnes,
moved, with the expectation of possibly spending
the night.

Later in the afternoon it was announced that the
relief party were coming and would soon reach us.
The first gentleman who appeared was Doctor
Cowan, from Mora, on a velocipede. He was followed by other kind friends from the same place,
who handed in package after package of delicious
and substantial eatables, canned meats and fruits,
coffee, sugar, crackers, cheese, dried beef, bacon,
canned fish and a generous supply of bread. This
was but a hint of the kindness and generosity which

it was our lot to receive from the good people of
Mora, our neighboring town, twelve miles away.

Kind Dr. Cowan came at once into our car and
with bandages and liniments ministered to the doctor and others whose eyes needed care. Then
mounting again his train velocipede, he hastened
away toward Hinckley.

So soiled and unkempt and discolored were we,
that I, at least, would gladly have kept out of sight,
but Mr. Ward being appointed distributor of the
stores, and requesting me to assist, the generous
supplies were soon handed to those in both cars, all
faring alike, and a good comfortable meal was the
portion of each.

"We can take some of you back with us," said
our new friends, who had two hand cars and a push
car, on which Mr. Nelson and family were already
seated.

Doctor and wife announced their determination
to remain where they were; "the princess" and the
two boys would remain too, with Maidie, who
wished to cast her lot for the present with her friend
and cousin. An opportunity was given to the Jewish women, who had little ones that were sick, as
was the case with some, to go too. As all wished
to go, or none, my husband and myself with Allen
and "the whooping coughers," as my sister called
them, with Mrs. Frame and her younger boys

embarked, after tying cloths about the children's heads to protect them from the cool air.

So, surrounded by kind and sympathizing friends, this forlorn party went on to Mora, reaching there after dark. On the way, one of our friends jumped off the car and ran up a steep bank, bringing back with him the large bag of cranberries gathered by Mabel and Alice Nelson the afternoon of the fire, and left by them on the outskirts ot the burned district. Though we had to get off, while the men carried our hand cars around the burned ties and bridges, in places, we went on with lightened hearts to a friendly reception in the pleasant and hospitable town of Mora.

CHAPTER IX.

THROUGH MANY DANGERS.

"Will you tell me what happened from the time you left your home until we saw you, after our own escape from the terrible fire?" I said to "the princess," when opportunity presented some time later.

"I will try and do the best I can," said she. "About two o'clock we noticed how badly smoked up the sky was. It looked almost as if it might be an eclipse of the sun, the smoke made it look so red. It kept getting worse and worse, and mamma thought she better go up to the boarding house and see how things looked.

"She got as far as the school house, couldn't see the flames anywhere, so came back. I started to read a story to her, but we couldn't seem to fix our minds on it; we would look up every once in a while and say, 'Oh, how smoky it is getting.'

"Finally it got so bad that we thought we had better go again and see how things were. Just then Willie came, saying there was a fire near the mill. (Willie had been down by the box car with another boy and something made him think he had better leave and go home.) Carlton appeared a few minutes afterwards. We had sent him up to the store. Everything was in confusion up there, people were trying to get things out of their houses in hopes of saving them (the things).

"We started in the path that leads to the school house. Willie says, 'Come this way, if you want to see the fire.' We then went the path that leads to Mr. Nelson's. After we got past the creek, we noticed that the woods around the school house were all on fire.

I knew then there was no hope for our house to be saved. We all wanted to go different ways. Mamma thought we had better go up the railroad track, Carlton thought we had better go home and pack the things up, so we would be prepared when the fire came; I wanted to go up to Mr. Nelson's and see what they were going to do.

"We finally decided to go there. When we got there all was confusion, and they were trying to get their things out.

"I asked Mrs. Baty what to do; she said, "Go down to the creek," so we went. People kept coming from all directions to get to a place of refuge.

"We had been there about two minutes, when we were obliged to go in the water as the sparks began to catch on our clothes. When we were in the water it looked just like a cyclone of fire; anywhere you would look you would see nothing but fire.

"When the bridge was on fire we would go on

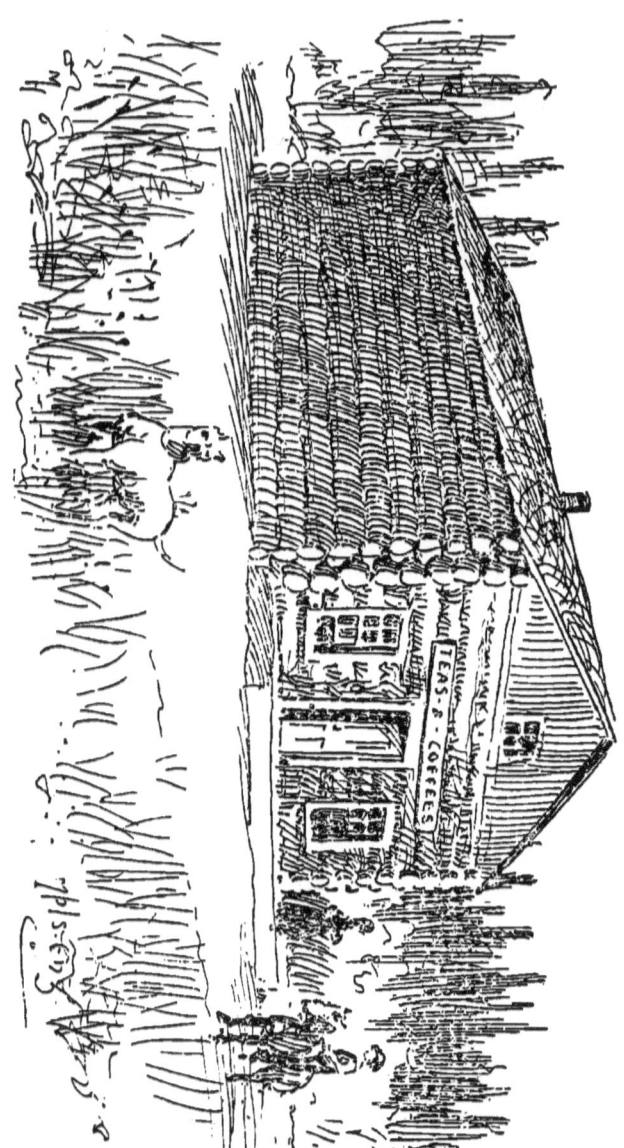

Mr. Berg's Store.

the opposite side of the creek, and when the mill was on fire, we went on the side where the bridge was. While we were in the creek, a cow came running down the bank and plunged head first into the water. It got where it was over its head and began to swim.

"We stayed till the fire had gone by (which seemed to be two or three hours) and then got out and had to dry our clothes on us. We had just been out a few moments when your folks came."

I learned that Mr. Braman, Seymour, Baty and others, got over fifty of the villagers into a deep pool two to four rods wide near the dam. The latter caught fire and blazed fiercely. On one side was the railroad bridge, one hundred and thirty feet long, and on the other, slabs and refuse lumber thrown over the bank, while just beyond was more than one hundred cords of hard wood and other lumber. The mill was not far away and the stables still nearer, so that they were completely encircled by terrible fires that burned furiously after the main blaze had swept onward. Across the bridge was a shallow pool where twenty-five people saved themselves in much the same way.

The water was so hot that the fish were found dead. It was here in the deeper pool that the drop of eighteen to twenty feet was known to be, and it was probably due to the heroic care of the men, that some of the women and children were saved from drowning.

Carlton's version of the fire, given in a letter to Meb, and dated Sept. 9th, will not be without interest:

Dear Sister Meb:

I expect you have read of the great fire that all the papers are talking about. I asked mamma what to write about and she said "Write about the fire," so I will tell you about it.

Right after dinner papa went out to Mr. Collier's to fight fire, so when the fire came papa was not with us. When it came I was up to the store. Willie was up to the depot, but when I came back Willie was there, and they were going to see about the fire.

As it happened we did not go to the school house, and when we got to the garden, the fire was burning the school house, so we escaped that way, but when we got to Mr. Nelson's all the people were excited, so we went to the pond just below the dam. The fire soon became too hot, so we went into the water and after a while all the things were burning around us, but we kept wet and were all right.

Papa ran through the fire with "Big Joe," but Joe got discouraged and didn't want to go further, but papa took him by the hand and so saved him.

From your loving brother,   .

CARLTON.

P. S.—Wasn't it funny about cousin Horace's box? He came up to Mora, Tuesday after the fire. Just as he got off the train, he saw us getting on. So he had the box put back on the train. The box was men's clothing, and when he found that papa and uncle had stayed in the burned district, he shipped it back *again* from Minneapolis.   C.

Asking my husband afterward how the fire looked to him, he replied: "When I was in the well the heat was so great above the well deck that I could not see except over head. When the fire was at its worst there was a cont'nuous flame above us.

"Just as I went into the well I took a glance about me. To the east the large trees caught fire in the top from the heated air. They burned with great fury. To the south and west there was a solid wall of fire that was like a furnace fire, and rolled up fifty feet at least and melted the trees as if they were wax candles.

"The house being of solid blocks burned a long time after the main fire had swept far beyond us, into the woods north."

I obtained from the doctor an account of his experience on that memorable afternoon. He also told me of the manner in which some of those who joined us on the following day were able to save themselves.

"John Powers, Mr. Thompson and Frank saved themselves by back-firing on a large meadow and putting wet blankets over themselves.   Mrs. Carver's daughter-in-law and two children were taken on the Eastern Minnesota train and taken back to Superior.

"We had cleared a piece of ground south of the box cars that were saved, with the stump puller. This and the burning over of this piece of land before, saved the cars.   Mr. Frame saved himself by reaching a piece of land that had been burned over before, and as it was on the edge of the fire, the heat was not sufficient to cause it to burn over again.

"We stayed by Mr. Collier's house, hoping to save it, till we were surrounded by the fire.   When the house burst into flames we jumped into a tub of water and poured water over each other; made a dash and were nearly overcome by the heat the first few rods; then the heat was not so intense, but painful to endure, and the smoke nearly suffocated us.

"After running about one hundred and twenty rods, all of us were obliged to lie down and bury our faces in our hands and the ground in order to breathe and rest from the suffocation and exhaustion.

"Soon after starting again I fell, and told Mr. Gonyea, who was behind me, to go on and save himself.   Mr. Collier had also gone on, and Mr. Chipris (Big Joe, as he was called,) and myself were left behind.   My companion became blind and could go no further, he thought. I took hold of his hand and led him.

"We succeeded in reaching the creek bed, and were filled with unspeakable thankfulness to God when we found that we could breathe, and that the heat was not so great as to endanger our lives further. I staid in the creek bed about three hours, then started up the creek leading "Big Joe" by the hand. I found Mrs. Frame and six children and Mrs. Braman in the creek bed about one mile above; left my blind companion with them, and after being started in a wagon road near them, felt my way home by keeping my right foot in the wagon track where I could feel the dust, and thus knew that I was in the road.

"I reached home at about 10:30, to find the village burned and my family and neighbors in the box cars."

The doctor and family and Maidie remained in the box car another twenty-four hours after we left them, my sister enjoying the luxury of a mattress that had been brought from Mora on the hand car. The others slept on bricks with insufficient covering, or none at all.

Pleasant surprise was theirs and our own, however, when one and another friend from distant points, during the following day made their appearance, rejoicing that the sad news they had received of disaster to the doctor's family and mine, was happily without ground.

The sad information came to us from time to time of those who perished on the first of September, eighteen hundred ninety-four, in our own settlement at Pokegama. Mr. Raymond's wife, three children, Mrs. Charles Anderson and her two children, and Mrs. Anderson's brother and sister Nora, were all found about one hundred rods northeast of Mr. Raymond's house. Charlie Olson was found about six rods from Mr. Molander's house. Mrs. Molander, her sister and two children were found about ten feet from the door of their house.

This information was given by the doctor three weeks after the fire. Further particulars came from J. D. Markham, of Rush City, of the firm of Kelsey & Markham, who owned the town site.

"We found Chas. Olson's body on Molander's farm and I assisted to bury it, with Mr. Molander's family, Anderson's and Raymond's, and Jay Braman.

"Mr. James Barnes' body was sent to St. Paul, and Erick Larson, the section man, was buried at Mora. Whitney and Goodsell's bodies not yet found, though persistent and frequent searches have been made. It is feared they were all burned up. There were no doubt twenty-three or twenty-four of ours burned up. Joseph Gonyea is in St.

Raphael's hospital in St. Cloud, feet and hands badly burned.

"All our burials were on Molander's place and Raymond's place. Mr. Braman assisted. All were put in decent boxes and funeral services held, with appropriate addresses given by Rev. Wm. Wilkinson, of Minneapolis, Episcopal clergyman of St. Andrew's church in that city, assisted by Rev. Fosbroke, of Sunrise, Minnesota, and Mr. Barnes, a divinity student of the Methodist church at Hamline, living at Milaca, all fine men and real workers, physical as well as spiritual.

"A cross of lath marks the grave of each unfortunate."

The same gentleman's account of the party of our neighbors who went on toward Hinckley the night of the fire, and the story of the efforts for the relief of those who remained over two nights in the burned district, have an interest peculiarly their own.

"Some remained in a coach and some in box cars, the coach was about two and one-half miles east of Pokegama, or five and a half miles from Hinckley. They got to Pine City Sunday afternoon. Mr. Carver and his wife reunited at the dam at Brook Park, or Pokegama."* (The elder Mr. Carver had gone up to Hinckley the day of the fire, with his daughter-in-law and two children on their way home

---

*Brook Park and Pokegama are the same, the post office being Brook Park.

to Wyoming. We heard later that his son after the fire, was searching for wife and children, and did not know for many days that they were taken in safety to Superior.)

"Mr. Braman gave up his wife as burned, but later she was brought to the coach, where they were again together.

"Mr. Seymour was only blinded from heat and smoke, and had to be led about for a few days.

"Mr. Baty and family went on to La Crosse, but Mr. Baty, senior, is now at Brook Park, at work building.

"Mr. Berg's family came on here, (to Rush City) Sunday afternoon, when we took them to my house, where with the aid of our good ladies here, they were clothed and made comfortable. Mr. Berg and Willie returned to Brook Park, while Mrs. Berg and children went to St. Paul to friends. They are now at Brook Park in a cabin of their own; went last Friday.

"The first hand car that went in from Hinckley Sunday, was of Rush City young men. They carried the car over burned bridges, etc., and took a can of milk. Their names are Geo. Knight, Gust. Lindgren, Grant Smith, W. S. Chapin, and B. O'Leary, I believe, and possibly others. They brought out the people from the coach, and some went a second trip back to the box cars.

"On the Monday night, Sept. 3d, I started with a

party and a hand car, from Hinckley. We had
thirty pairs of blankets, one barrel of bread, six
planks, a good tent and poles, three shovels, one
spade, one axe, one saw, one pick-axe, one water
pail, two lanterns, three satchels, three lunch baskets
and the personal extras of the party, also a cedar
post. Starting at 6:15 P. M., got to box cars at
Pokegama just before 1 A. M., had to leave the
car at the east side of the trestle bridge, beyond the
dam, and carry blankets, etc., nearly a mile to the
box cars, where we found people cold, and covered,
some with wet clothes, others with nothing.

"We slept (or tried to) from about 2 to 5 A. M.
We made ten or fifteen transfers of the hand car,
always unloading and reloading except in a few
instances we got over by aid of the post as a roller
under the car. We had a long transfer around the
wrecked train, also at one bridge, to go round, had
to shovel fire and ashes to get through, with a terrific wind blowing, and dangerous looking, I can
assure you.

"The party were Dr. H. B. Allen, Cloquet; Dr.
C. W. Higgins, Minneapolis; Rev. Wm. Wilkinson,
of the same city; B. J. Kelsey, Kenyon, of our
firm; Rev. Fosbroke, of Sunrise Minn., (Episcopal);
Mr. Alex Berg, Mr. Thompson, of New Brighton,
Minn., (brother of our Mr. Thompson); W. W.
Braman and myself. It was an awful experience.

Joe Coblin's poor log shanty four miles southeast, is the only house in our settlement not burned."

Capt. W. P. Allen, of the C. N. Nelson Lumber Company, of Cloquet, Minn., started shortly after his brother Dr. Allen did, with a trunk of clothing. Leaving the train at Pine City, he rode twenty-eight miles across the country to Mora, only to find his two sisters and their families gone to New Brighton and Cloquet. Promising to send lumber and men from Cloquet to build a house for his brother-in-law, C. W. Kelsey, he returned to help care for those who preceded him.

Thanks to the generosity of the Relief Committee, backed by hundreds of sympathizing friends, who showed in this time of utter need, their sympathy in substantial ways, many of those who survived have returned to the settlement at Brook Park, or will return when houses are ready for them.

Already fully a dozen married men are hard at work, preparing shelter for their families, besides five or six single men, while carpenters and masons from Cloquet and Minneapolis, and a civil engineer from Minneapolis, who is surveying lots and lands, are on the ground, with Rev. Mr. Wilkinson's son in charge. One man has gone to St. Paul to bring back his family.

Parties from South Dakota are coming in to make a permanent home. Ten houses are now under way, or will soon be commenced. Work has commenced on a new school house, and it is hoped school will begin in one month.

"All are in a hustle of work with the first house, (that given by Capt. W. P. Allen) rushing up, as the best and most substantial in it or in Hinckley, so far," writes one who was on the ground at an early date, after the fire.

CHAPTER X.

THE GREATER HOLOCAUST.

The reader has thus far been led by familiar
sketches of the people of one settlement and vicinity,
to enter to some extent into the experiences of those
who on one day were quietly and happily pursuing
their usual avocations, and the next were thrown
into dismay and misery by the ruin of home and
property. To this was added the unspeakable
anguish caused by the conviction that there were
many of their friends and neighbors, who had passed
through the fiery furnace of flames, and, in one
moment were beyond help.

If the thought of a score of human lives going
out in a fearful agony of pain, is heart-rending, lan-
guage fails when we contemplate the fact that on
that first day of September, eighteen hundred and
ninety-four, hundreds were cut down remorselessly
in more thickly settled communities lying in the
wake of this devastating conflagration.

The overflowing cup of horror is full to the very
brim. Little children, sprightly youth, men and
women in their prime and the gray-haired, were
swept out of life in that seething tempest of wind and
flame, while hundreds of homes and the accumula-
tions of years were engulfed in the common

ruin. In neighboring towns, miles and miles away, the shadow of presentiment darkened the skies, and filled with apprehension the hearts of those who felt assured that something of terrible import was happening. Some even believed that the end of the world was at hand.

At four o'clock the darkness of night seemed approaching, telegraphic communications were cut off, and only vague rumors hinted of the dreadful holocaust soon to be revealed in all its magnitude.

All too soon tangible reports confirmed the flying rumors. Hinckley, and adjacent towns on the St. Paul & Duluth and on the Eastern Minnesota, were completely wiped out.

After noon of that memorable day, the wind, already strong, had become a hurricane, and forest fires that had been smoldering for weeks joined and swept forward as one, with resistless fury. Two hundred men had been fighting fire on the outskirts of the town of Hinckley.

No human power could stop it now. All fled for their lives, abandoning completely the hope of saving property of any description. In the terrible race, hundreds were mown down and hundreds more would have perished, had it not been for the heroism of those brave men whose names will go down to posterity as heroes of the hour.

The St. Paul & Duluth (Limited), making the run from Duluth with Sullivan, conductor, and James Root,

engineer, entered a belt of land where the smoke
was so dense that one could not see his hand before
him.   The smoke cleared, and they reached a point
two to three miles from Hinckley about 3 p. m.
Here people rushed toward the train from all directions, to the number of one hundred and twenty-
five, shouting, "Hinckley is being burned to cinders!
For God's sake, save us!"

These people were taken on the train, swelling
the passenger list to nearly two hundred and sixty.
The engineer says, "I could see no fire then, but all
of a sudden the wind came with a rush.   As I
stepped into my cab everything seemed to be a ball
of fire.   It was as sudden as a flame bursting from
a lamp."

The train was now on blaze from end to end, the
engineer's clothes on fire, the thick panes in the
coach windows bursting with heat and smashing in
pieces, the passengers wild with fear, some throw-
ing themselves from the train.   Those who remained
were taken to the vicinity of a swamp, and leaving
the fated train made a rush for their lives and
reached the slush and mud in Skunk Lake, which
proved to them a haven of refuge.   Here they remained all night; help reached them in the morning from Pine City, and they were at last conveyed
to Duluth and Superior.

The heroic conductor, Sullivan, remained at his
post, calm and collected, while many of the passen-

gers were losing their senses. But when the worst
was over, and the train lay a ruined mass of smoking debris, one and a half miles south of Sandstone,
Sullivan broke down, and later was taken to a hospital to recover his shattered reason.

"Our escape was entirely due to the thoughtful-
ness and heroic efforts of Engineer Root, sustained
by his brave fireman," is the unqualified assertion of
one of the passengers. The noble man was terribly
burned during the retrograde flight from the fire, at
one time fainting away.

Not less striking, was the courage and high sense
of fidelity to duty, shown by the conductor and engineer of the Eastern Minnesota, which, leaving
Superior early in the afternoon, reached Hinckley
in its hour of need. These noble men held the train,
the caboose and five freight cars were hastily detached
from the way freight, a portion of which was on fire.
Attaching these cars to the passenger train, room
was afforded for a large number.

Engineer Best stood at his post; the town was
now swept by billows of fire, and the flame-pursued
people rushed to the train and were helped on board
to the number of four to five hundred.

Conductor Powers acted the hero throughout the
whole catastrophe. He uncoupled the engine from
the train, crossed a burning trestle with it, to get
the freight cars, hauled them back, then calming the
fears of crazed women and children, hurried all on

the train and holding his train till the last minute, carried it across burning bridges, over tracks where the ties were a fire, and the rails liable to warp and dash the train to destruction, out to safety, through heat so terrific as to be almost insufferable, and through smoke so dense as to obscure everything except the horror on every side.*

This train passed safely through, reaching Duluth at about 9:20 that night, where the large number saved were cared for by the noble generosity of the people of that city.

Engineer Best in describing the situation says, "After leaving Superior at 1:15 P. M., I had to light the head light, owing to the dense smoke that turned day into night. The smoke and heat increased as we approached Hinckley. I expected that when we reached that point we would get into the open and escape from the smoke. My surprise was great therefore, when we found the fire right upon the town. It took but a glance to see that the town was doomed. The wind blew with great velocity, and the flames fairly leaped through the air. The people were taken by surprise and were terrorized and helpless. The coming of the fire seemed like a stroke of lightning.

"Away we went through the blazing woods, and may be we didn't fly. The telegraph posts and the

---

*We are indebted to Twin City and Duluth papers for these facts.

ties were on fire and a stream of flame passed under the train. The people were packed so closely in the train that it was impossible to move. We passed several bridges that were on fire. At Partridge we stopped and procured water for the passengers. The fire was roaring behind us then. Within half an hour the fire had reached Partridge. This fact gives an idea of how fast the flames traveled.

"We all drew a sigh of relief when we reached the limits of Superior and knew our precious freight was safe."

At the northwestern edge of Hinckley was the mill pond. On its bank stood the plant of the Brennan Lumber Co. and its yard, with about half a million feet of sawed lumber. Many were seen on their way to this pond, but none returned.

A special to the Duluth *News-Tribune* says: "Your correspondent has viewed to-day (Sept. 2d) three hundred and twelve separate dead bodies and there are many others he has been unable to reach."

Many were so completely incinerated that they could not be identified. There were other towns totally wiped out. Mission Creek, Miller, Sandstone, Pokegama, afterwards called Brook Park, and adjacent territory swell the sorrowful list. In Sandstone four or five hundred people were left homeless, while more than half a hundred are numbered among the burned. Of outlying districts the whole truth may never be known.

Great honor is due to those who carefully sought
and interred the bodies of the dead, many of whom
were buried where they fell, while others were
placed in trenches or wells.   Orders were to carefully preserve anything which might lead to identi-
fication, and to mark the graves and make a careful
note of their location.

The death roll has never been called and perhaps
never will, as many took refuge in the quarries near
Sandstone, some in Kettle River in a deep gorge,
while others in wells, died a death which was a mix-
ture of drowning, suffocating and burning.

It is a picture too sad to dwell on long. From the
universal sorrow some found cause for joy and
thankfulness; joy, that those they believed dead were
safe, and in time were restored to them; thankfulness, that though in many cases property was all
swept away, yet dear ones, whole families in many
cases, passed through the fiery ordeal unscarred.

With pleasure we record the countless instances
of heroism, self-sacrifice and helpfulness in individu-
al cases and the noble generosity of the people at
large.

It has been truly said "That such a condition should
touch the hearts of the commonwealth was but
natural, and from every part of the country came
spontaneous relief. Men who had hitherto been
miserly, gave freely of their gold; presidents of
soul-less corporations gave thousands of dollars;

food and clothing came from thousands of homes, and even prattling school children collected coppers to add to the fund." The statement that "the economic loss resulting from these great forest fires will reach into the millions, but as yet no computation of it is possible," is no doubt true.

Many who were enjoying prosperity and were surrounded by the comforts and luxuries of life, to-day find themselves, thanks to the generosity of the people, possessed indeed of the necessaries of life; yet the change is great.

A few, by the equal and impartial distribution of funds through wise and reliable committees, are lifted perhaps from squalor and poverty to a fair condition.

By far the greater number probably, begin life anew, under comparatively unfavorable circumstances. Yet to these there is hope that out of this seemingly great loss, will come an improved condition in years to come.

This great conflagration has swept away a vast amount of wooded growth which must in time have been cleared by the incessant toil of the pioneer.

The very ashes will form a fertilizer which will enrich the soil, now transformed into a vast agricultural district. There still remains in sections at least, wood that may be utilized as fuel, and the ground will be much more easily cleared and seeded than before this would have been possible.

These great fires will not be without valuable
results in waking up the people to the need of protecting in the future the vast wooded districts of the
country from a repetition of this calamity. Already
means have been discussed in the St. Paul Confer-
ence early in October.

Plans are being outlined for the prevention of such
fires, and the encouragement of forestry. Stringent
laws will be enforced. Thus in the years to come,
it may be said that from "The September Holocaust," have risen monuments that shall be a lasting
glory and benefit to the American people.

CHAPTER XI.

AFTERMATH.

A trip through the burned district on the 27th of October brings us to Hinckley, rapidly being rebuilt. All is alive with activity. New dwellings are springing up as by magic, while larger business blocks are taking shape. There were reported at that time one hundred and fifty-four new buildings at Hinckley and vicinity. About thirty more will be built this fall. The Eastern Minnesota has erected a new depot, which is now nearly completed.

Beyond the St. Paul & Duluth tracks may be found the long building containing the stores of the relief committee. Here may be seen piles of clothing of every size and description, supplies for table and all necessary articles for household use. By printed cards the applicants receive orders on this department, and all pressing wants are supplied by the kind friends who represent the committee here. The intention is to treat all with like consideration.

The station of the St. Paul & Duluth road is a low frame building close by the track. We saw a woman there talking with the agent and her eyes were overflowing. They were not the only tears shed that day, as incident after incident was brought to our knowledge of those among the survivors who failed to find their friends, or suffered from subsequent effects of the strain of September first. One family was specially noticeable at that time. There was such a drawn look of suffering visible upon the mother's face that a lady near me suggested that she might be suffering from sick headache, offering a lemon for her relief.

Going to the group I inquired of the mother, who held her youngest on her lap, if she were suffering. "Yes," she answered, "and I have been sick ever since the fire."

She with her family had escaped on the train, and her four little children, warmly and prettily clad, gave evidence of the kind generosity they had met with at Duluth. They were now on their way to Rutledge, where a new home awaited her, but the look on her face told volumes of what she had been through and of her present unfitness to care for her little family. There was a look of patient gratitude on her husband's face, and both showed pleasure at our interest in their sad case.

Near this station was a temporary eating house, and small white tents dotted the ground near by, while the ruined walls of a large brick school house loomed in the background.

It seemed strange indeed to see the buildings of the Eastern Railway intact—water tanks, coal sheds, round house, etc.,—while all about, the ground was ploughed up by the fire, trees divested of their leaves bending toward the ground, some of them quite prostrate, though not uprooted, and a few rods away were the ruins of a building, the stove shattered, the cellar yawning.

"Oh," we thought, "if the people had only known, they might have run to these buildings and their vicinity for shelter."

That the fire and wind on September first was indeed of the nature of a cyclone, was demonstrated in many ways. The fact that the fire jumped from place to place was beyond controversy. At Hinckley, a trunk that was carried across some of the tracks of the St. Paul & Duluth, was unharmed, though everything was melted not fifty yards away. The trees at Pokegama were bent in most places toward the northeast, yet in places a few rods away there were seen some turned in the opposite direction.

Mr. Berg, at Pokegama, thinking he could save his house, watched the fire and only gave up hope of rescuing his property when the house was ignited. He said the fire flashed through the air in a moment's time, and did not reach the house by way of the trees or the grass near. He had tried to persuade his wife to remain, as he thought the house perfectly protected.

Scores of trees were uprooted and these with the light earth clinging to the roots, formed perpendicular walls which faced in different directions.

Mrs. Meyers of Barnum, told me that they lighted

lamps at that place at 3:30 P. M., and for weeks had
holes dug in the ground in which to take refuge.
Some of her neighbors thought the last day had real-
ly come, though little realizing at the time, that it
was indeed the last day to so many.

The depot agent at Hinckley telegraphed to
Rutledge, "We are surrounded by fire, I must go,"
making a rush for his life.

Two young ladies by the name of Gunn, were
many hours under water; being unwilling at first to
submerge themselves, they were held down by a
kind friend who realized their great peril.

It was reported that the mill pond at Hinckley
was drained after the fire, and one hundred and fifty
bodies were found. On the fatal day, a blind man,
and an invalid who was unable to rise from a roller
chair, were saved, while others less helpless dropped
by the way.

So strong was the wind, that trees were heard
falling in the woods half an hour or more before the
fire swept through.

While waiting for the train at Hinckley, I met
Mr. Baty on his way home to Wisconsin, to remain.
So in the voyage of life, some favoring wind brings
in sight a familiar sail which we signal gladly and
pass, knowing not whether we shall ever see it
again on this side the harbor bar.

He told me that only that morning had the body
of Fred Molander been found in a well on his own

place. Mr. Baty's theory was, that returning to find his wife and children beyond hope, he hurried into the well near his house, which caved in on him, shutting off his last hope of rescue. The bodies first supposed to be those of Mr. Anderson and Mr. Molander, were those of Mr. Whitney and Mr. Goodsell, and no trace had yet been found of Mr. Anderson.

Many incidents only too true, that would have interested all and touched each heart, have been omitted from this record. Space and time forbid the telling of much that would speak loudly of heroism, fortitude and endurance, both on the part of those who lived through the hours so fraught with suffering and danger, and of the friends who through stupendous difficulties, forced their way to the relief of those who were in so great peril.

To the railroad companies who furnished free transportation to the fire sufferers, grateful acknowledgements are offered. The expense of repairing roads to these companies was very great. One bridge over Kettle River on the Eastern Minnesota required fifteen days for repairs. In passing from Hinckley to Mora the number of new bridges and culverts give proof of the extensive repairs necessary on this road after the fire. Men are still at work putting in new ties and leveling the tracks.

To the doctors who rendered such kind and efficient aid throughout those trying times, faithful friends who were first to come and last to go, such reward as comes from hearts full of gratitude is and ever shall be yours.

To every one who contributed to the relief of the unfortunates, either great sums or small, the universal sentiment of those who had a share in this largess must be, God bless you now and always. To those who at Pine City, St. Cloud, notably at Duluth, the Twin Cities and many other points nobly gave in countless ways to lighten and relieve the burdens of the homeless refugees, the wish of grateful hearts must ever be, God grant you like succor in time of need. Surely such scenes as these bring all together in ties of universal brotherhood.

    *   *   *   *   *   *

The winter is fast approaching. Happily the pure, white snow will soon cover from view much of the desolation and ruin the great forest fire has wrought. In the coming spring time, the new grass will veil to some extent, traces of this great conflagration.

Sorrowing hearts will sadly cherish the memory of those whose lives were offered up a sacrifice. Time, the great healer, however, will chasten this sorrow, and those who mourn will learn to look beyond the grave and hope for a happy reunion with loved ones. The years will soon pass and smiling, prosperous farms and towns will stretch themselves over the land where ruin once held its brief carnival.

It is hard to quench the spark of hope in the heart of man. God kindly wills it so, for while toil rewards the willing hand,

"There's a good time coming."

The kind generosity of uncounted numbers have made it possible for those who suffered the loss of home and property at Hinckley, Sandstone, Mission Creek, Miller, Pokegama and the adjacent territory, to take heart and begin life anew. The noble list of contributions has swelled to *over one hundred thousand dollars.*

To the writer, this record would not be complete with simply a passing tribute to the people of Mora, whose kindness in great things and in small, cheered and helped those who from first to last they treated as brothers, sisters and friends.

Of the kind doctors, ministers, men and women, as well as children there, who had a part in this noble work, not even the names can appear, but all of us who received of their kindness of heart and hand, will surely unite in commending them to Him who said: "I was an hungered and ye gave me meat; I was thirsty and ye gave me drink; I was a stranger and ye took me in; naked and ye clothed me; I was sick and ye visited me. * * * *

Verily, I say unto you; inasmuch as ye have done it unto one of the least of these my brethren, ye have done it unto me."

THE END.

www.ingramcontent.com/pod-product-compliance
Lightning Source LLC
Chambersburg PA
CBHW020751020726
47495CB00008B/2370